Jenalee Storm:
Magic Endures

Novel #2 of The Dark Crossing Trilogy

Raven Aren James

Books by Raven Aren James:
- Jenalee Storm: Magic Rises (the first novel of *The Dark Crossing Trilogy*)
- Jenalee Storm: Magic Endures
- Jenalee Storm: Magic Returns

Praise for *Jenalee Storm*
- "Raven Aren James brings real **humor** and **excitement** to the writing of the *Jenalee Storm Trilogy*." – Linda Chappo, author

- "*The Jenalee Storm Trilogy* is action-packed and very well written. Once you start reading the first book, you won't be able to put it down and will crave to read the next books in this fun and exciting trilogy." – Veronica Wagenet, writer

Also by Raven Aren James
Read the Whole Trilogy:

 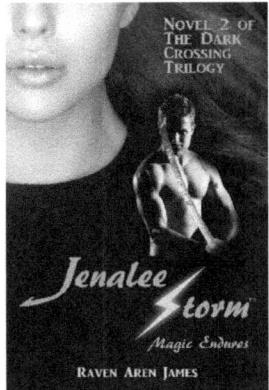 

Jenalee Storm and her mentor, Jack AngelSword, face a whole universe of vampires, werewolves, demons, dragons and unspeakable evil.

Here's your chance to get access to **Behind-the-Scenes fun.** When you **subscribe** to the exclusive enewsletter:

- **See Exclusive Artwork** (from the upcoming graphic novels)
- **Discover details** about movement toward a television series and/or feature films
- **Get Early Access** to announcements about upcoming books, graphic novels, merchandise and more related to Jenalee Storm and her friends.

Subscribe at JenaleeStorm.com/subscribe

CONTENTS

DEDICATION AND ACKNOWLEDGEMENTS

This book is dedicated to you, the reader—and the team that brought it together.

This book also dedicated to the terrific Video/Audio Strategist and author Johanna E. Mac Leod.

Thanks to Johanna E. Mac Leod for her guidance all along the way for the Jenalee Storm trilogy and for the books' covers. Thanks to Kevin Trivedi, Jonathan J. Colton David MacDowell Blue, Dave Thude, Linda Chappo and Charles Hall for listening to portions of the material and for providing guidance related to the text and to the books' covers. Thanks to Jen Averre for guidance related to the text and covers. Thanks to Kalen Vavla, the coach who encouraged my novel writing.

Thanks to Barry Adamson II for editing sections of the material. Thanks to Judita Bacinskaite who encouraged me to look for an overall pattern for the covers.

Thanks to other friends who listened as I read all three novels aloud: Mark Clark, Veronica Wagenet, Mike Lamonthe, Bob Choat, Andrew Weiss, Marc Levine, Niko Pope, Benson Wong, and Robert Evans Wilson, Jr.

Thanks to my parents, friends, team members, students and clients—all along the way. Thank you to Higher Power. Many great moments to you all – *Raven Aren James*

Chapter 1

I gasped as I saw my friend, Jack AngelSword, get cut by Trin's sword. That had to hurt terribly. Blood must be pouring down his arm from the wound on his shoulder. I couldn't see much because I stood at ground level, and Jack moved precariously on a top ledge of the bell tower in Venice, Italy.

"Team! I've located Jack. He's in trouble. Let's run to the tower," I said.

"Jenalee, you mean St. Mark's Campanile—?" Daniel called back over the comm line.

"Exactly. Jack's battling Trin at the top—"

I dashed across St. Mark's Square, glancing to my left and right. If only I could have sent Marta, the vampire, to assist Jack, but she was still healing on board the Helios airship.

I realized that Sahkeisha and Elyse had more distance to cover. They weren't here yet.

"Daniel, send up your drone. Get eyes on the situation. You might even be able to do something to help Jack."

"On it," Daniel said.

"I'm entering the bell tower—" I replied. Inside the building, I saw a line of people and the doors of the elevator closing. Normally, I'd never jump ahead. I'd like to punch people who cut lines.

But, with Jack's life at stake, courtesy be damned. Give me a break, an emergency calls for extreme measures. I'll take a pass on this one.

I barely managed to get into the elevator as the doors closed.

"Daniel, what do you see?" I called him via our commlink. The people on board the elevator glared at me.

"I—oh, no! Trin's stabbed Jack through the gut, and he's done the same to her with his AngelSword," Daniel said, reporting what he could see on his monitor. Evidently the drone floated high up near the top of St. Mark's Campanile.

"It's horrible. Wait! They're glowing. So bright. I can't—"

Damn this slow elevator! Slow as shit in molasses. Jack needs me and—

Finally, the elevator doors opened.

Trin, an Asian, lithe-figured woman, kneeled on the floor, as she tied the hilt of her sword in such a way that no one could draw the sword without going through a lot of trouble. This sword had a vicious reputation—the Sword of the Dark Bloom.

Before anyone could get off the elevator, I hit the down button, jumped out, and said, "Excuse me!"

I heard the people groan as the elevator car descended.

I looked back at Trin. Her head was still tilted down, which caused her hair to veil her face.

I wasn't looking forward to her lifting her face. The last time I saw her—the Demon that lives in the Sword of the Dark Bloom had gauged out her left eye.

"Where's Jack?" I yelled.

"He's gone," Trin said.

"Did you knock him over the ledge?" I asked. I didn't trust her worth spit—so I went to the window and looked down, seeing the ground about 300 feet below. No body. Jack had not fallen to his death.

I looked back at Trin. I felt shock at what I saw.

Her face ... her left eye had returned—fully healed.

Her face had no bruises, no injuries.

What the hell happened? And what had taken Jack away?

Did that bright glow abduct Jack to someplace else—maybe, some other dimension?

Chapter 2

My rage at Trin, like fire in my veins, powered my hands. I released my fighting sticks from the holsters beneath my arms. I snapped them open, so they doubled in length.

"Tell me where Jack is. Tell me now or I'll use these sticks to loosen your tongue and your teeth," I said. Pretty lame — that last sentence. So, I was pissed, and falling into .... What? A pirate cliché?

"I don't know," Trin said.

"You don't know? You stabbed him, you goddammed bitch!"

I wasn't being smart. Trin wielded her sword better than my own mentor, Jack AngelSword. Worse. She excelled as a sorceress who could just wave her hand, toss a burst of energy and slam me into a wall. I threatened her like a sardine would threaten a great white shark.

Trin remained seated, kneeling on the floor.

Click.

I tensed up, bracing myself for something.

What happened surprised me. Apparently, Trin released the strap on her other sword scabbard. Now both of her swords were on the floor.

"I surrender," Trin said.

At that moment, Sahkeisha strode out of the elevator—I caught her form with my peripheral vision.

"Tree her," I said.

"What?" Sahkeisha asked.

"Oh—for the love of—use one of your tangle-tree magic bulbs on her," I said.

"Right." Sahkeisha tossed a bulb near Trin. The bulb exploded, and tree limbs rose up and ensnarled Trin.

"Is this really a good idea?" Sahkeisha asked. Her eyebrow rose, and a bit of a smile graced her chocolate-tinted face.

That's when I got her meaning.

This tangle-tree around Trin meant one thing. We were going to have a hell of a time getting Trin into the elevator.

I pressed a couple of keys in my pocket comm device, basically shifting the comm line frequency so I could reach Mrs. Chi.

"Mrs. Chi. We have Trin," I said. "Please bring the Helios to St. Mark's Campanile. Trin has surrendered. We need to make a quick exit."

"Roger that. Captain Yang bring us about," Mrs. Chi said.

* * * * * *

Using a few choice spells, we freed Trin from the magical tangle-tree, and we made the tree disappear from the floor of St. Mark's Campanile.

Captain Yang sent the Helios elevator car down to us. While the Helios hovered, we stepped from the ledge at the top of St. Mark's Campanile into the elevator car.

The elevator car opened on the Central level of the airship. Mrs. Chi took one look at Trin and exclaimed, "Trin! Your eye—it's healed."

"Mom—it's good to see you," Trin said.

Mrs. Chi and Trin embraced. Mother and daughter at peace for once.

Sahkeisha and I looked on, surprised.

While the reunion took place, Ensign Esperanza, taking her cue from Captain Yang, sent the elevator back down to retrieve Daniel and Elyse.

Meanwhile, I glared at Trin.

"Yeah. Great. Happy reunion. Remember, Mrs. Chi—Trin stabbed Jack. And he's missing. Unlike *little-Miss-I'm-happy-to-see-you-Mom*—Jack has always been loyal. He's always been trustworthy," I said. Yeah, bitterness dripping on each word.

Trin took a big breath. Her eyes downcast. "Like me, Jack returned from the Ethereal Plane—free of physical injury. But things are worse."

"Worse—what?" I asked.

"The Cross of Sighs—it took hold of his right forearm—like a leech. Wherever Jack is—I fear for him," Trin said.

"You stab Jack with the Sword of the Dark Bloom and you sic the Cross of Sighs on him, too?!" I lunged toward Trin. Mrs. Chi moved fast, with grace, and simply guided me to the side.

It must have been Aikido.

"Mrs. Chi! You can't let her have free run of this ship. Because of her, my friends almost died," I said.

"What—" Mrs. Chi said, quietly. "—would you have me do?"

"Put her in the brig. There's a jail on this ship, right?"

Mrs. Chi took a breath.

"I'll go," Trin offered up her wrists, gesturing that she would accept cuffs.

"That's not necessary. Ensign Esperanza—" Mrs. Chi said.

"Yes, Ma'am." Ensign Esperanza stepped forward—her

actions with a snap to them.

Mrs. Chi nodded.

Ensign Esperanza guided Trin to the elevator.

Trin looked back to me with regret in her eyes.

Regret? Damn right, she should have regret.

Mrs. Chi looked at me. She looked like she had some level of peace. How did she do that?

"She's your daughter. It's your job to forgive her," I said.

"As a leader, you must learn when to guide, when to be stern and when to forgive."

I shook my head. "Some things are unforgivable."

"So quick to judge," Mrs. Chi said. "Join me in my office. Nine minutes."

"I'm sure you know the quote from Mahatma Gandhi," Mrs. Chi said, as she sat back in her chair. Her office matched her. Tidy. Stern. And spare. I sat on the edge of my chair—not comfortable.

"About forgiveness?"

"Yes. Gandhi said, "The weak can never forgive. Forgiveness is the attribute of the strong."

I took a breath. "I don't feel that strong."

"I like to say, 'Only the strong can forgive," Mrs. Chi said.

"I don't want to forgive." I began. "I'm supposed to lead my people—to get something done. If I can't trust Trin, I can't have her be on *my* team. How do I know that she won't get angry again and hurt somebody else on this team? I can't take that risk."

"Every human being makes big mistakes," Mrs. Chi said. "Things that they regret. Now, we don't know what exactly happened. Trin says that some force pushed her arm to stab Jack. I'm inclined to believe her. Because she has not been a person to tell lies. She's disagreed with me when she was younger. She rebelled, but she did not tell lies."

"I don't have any good history with Trin," I said. "All I know is that every time that Jack asked her to share the Silent Scepter, she refused. All I know is that she can be obsessive. She can be cruel."

"We also know something else," Mrs. Chi said. "As a warrior and a sorceress, Trin could have killed Jack multiple times. She can restrain herself."

"I don't know what that means. Maybe she's just sweet on him. He seems to be having the same effect on that vampire, Marta. Maybe Trin just has the hots for Jack, and that's why she didn't kill him."

Mrs. Chi frowned.

"How can I make the right decision as a leader when I don't have enough information, and the only information I do have is that Trin is unreliable?"

"A leader must rely on intuition and experience," Mrs. Chi began. "We never have enough data. There is research that shows that intuition is data that has not risen to the conscious level."

"I don't see how that helps me," I said.

A knock at Mrs. Chi's office door.

"Enter."

Dr. Lethem, a fit, sturdy woman, probably just under 50 years old, stepped in and closed the door behind her.

Dr. Lethem sat down. We were now in a sort of triangle. I noted how Mrs. Chi did not hide behind her desk.

"I want you to hear this directly from Dr. Lethem. She impresses me. There is something to learn from her," Mrs. Chi said.

"If this is about forgiving Trin, I'll just leave now," I said, rising from my chair.

"Tell her about your son," Mrs. Chi invited Dr. Lethem to

speak.

"My son died. He was 15 years old. You should have seen him—seen my Andy," Dr. Lethem began.

I sat back down.

Tears came to Dr. Lethem's eyes. "Andy was a good boy. Compassionate. Jumped to his feet to vacate his seat on the subway so an elderly person could sit down. He would have grown up strong and reliable. A good member of this crew—"

"I believe it to be so," Mrs. Chi said. She placed her hand on Dr. Lethem's shoulder.

"Andy was 15 years old when he was shot. Murdered by another 15-year-old," Dr. Lethem said.

I admit it. This shook me. Hell, I'm eighteen. I've only been on the planet three more years than Dr. Lethem's son. I liked those years. Well, much of them. When Gram-Gram was alive. *Oh, shit, I don't want to—*

"I know you lost your grandmother," Dr. Lethem said.

Now things were blurry. Tears in my eyes. Didn't want to go there.

"People said I did something—" Dr. Lethem said.

"Something ... noble," Mrs. Chi said.

"I testified and put that kid, Bobby, in prison," Dr. Lethem said.

I kept silent, listening.

"I visited Bobby. In the whole world, I was the only one who visited him in that prison."

"Nobody in his family?" I asked.

"He had an aunt. Two uncles. Three cousins. They couldn't be bothered."

"How...? How could you visit somebody who murdered—?"

"—my boy. I can't describe the rage I felt. My boy was

gone. The emptiness. I filled up with only rage. Yeah—I testified. I put that kid—that murderer—into prison. He deserved it. But it didn't do me much good. Nothing was bringing my boy, Andy, back." Dr. Lethem shook, the hurt fresh again.

"So, the kid, Bobby, who pulled the trigger—" Dr. Lethem began. "—he got 21 years no time off for good behavior. He'd be out when he turned 36. I read something. It said, 'Forgiveness is a release from a cycle of blame and suffering.' Just maybe I could fill the emptiness with something else. Maybe I might prevent the total loss of the second boy. Perhaps he could grow up—even in that prison—into a man who had integrated that awful first chapter. Maybe it would guide him to be a better man."

"Out at 36—"

"I visited him for two years."

I blinked.

"He died. Killed by another inmate," Dr. Lethem said. She shook her head.

"That year, I also lost my husband," Mrs. Chi said.

Dr. Lethem shuddered.

"I'm sorry for taking you through this, Dr. Lethem. I just feel that Jenalee would benefit—"

"I'm—I'm glad to help. We're one crew," Dr. Lethem said.

"That we are. That is all, Jenalee," Mrs. Chi said.

I rose. I bowed—the Asian sign of respect. It just felt natural. "Thank you, Mrs. Chi. Thank you, Dr. Lethem."

They both nodded once.

I closed the door behind me.

I walked down the corridor toward my room. I heard the muffled thrum of the Helios' engines.

Noah approached, smiled. Then he said, "That's it!"

"That's what?" I said.

"I understand now," Noah said.

I listened.

"Mrs. Chi is grooming you."

"Grooming me for what?" I said.

"To take over. To be her successor," Noah said.

"This makes no sense. Of course, she would train Jack to be her successor. I mean his name is AngelSword. This is the House of AngelSword."

"Right. And her name is Mrs. Chi AngelSword," Noah said.

"Don't be a wiseass."

"That's not the part of me that's wise."

We paused and stood there.

"Jenalee, let me be serious for a moment," Noah said. "Don't you notice we all follow you. Just take it as a sign from the universe. You're meant to lead us. You have been leading us. And Mrs. Chi is better than a wiseass. She's somebody full of wisdom."

Walking past, Mrs. Chi said, "Noah, that is one of your better observations."

* * * * * *

One hour later, the Helios hovered over the docks. But deep into the city, Dr. Lethem clung to the shadows. She glanced at her right hand—watched it elongate into a claw. Dr. Lethem stretched her now wolf-shoulders. The same year she lost her "second son" Bobby, she had been turned into a werewolf.

She did everything to hide her nature from Mrs. Chi and the crew.

At the street corner, Dr. Lethem snarled as she saw a

street thug pistol whip a shop owner, visible through a convenience store window.

The street thug strutted out of the store, putting the cash from the till in his pocket. The thug smiled.

Going to wipe that smile off your face, asshole, Dr. Lethem thought. Giving full expression to the Beast in her.

She bounded across the dark street. Her turn—she slapped the back of her claw against the thug's face, knocking him into the wall between shops.

"What? What are you?"

"Death," Dr. Lethem said.

She tore off the thug's right arm which had moments before moved to pistol whip the shop owner.

Dr. Lethem thoroughly enjoyed the sensation of her claws slicing through human flesh. It made all the risks worth it. With her massive wolf-jaws, Dr. Lethem tore most of the thug's throat away, leaving his head attached to his torso by his spine.

Delicious.

"You seem to be enjoying yourself," Sable Cane said as she stepped forward out of the shadows.

Dr. Letham turned and gathered herself, just about to spring.

Sable waved her hand, and Sable's burst of magical energy tossed Dr. Lethem into a nearby streetlamp pole.

"No. I wouldn't try to force the issue. Listen. And listen well. You know who I am?"

"Sable Cane."

"Good. Trying to deceive me would have been foolish. However, you've been in the deceiving business for some time now—aboard Mrs. Chi's airship."

"What do you want?" Dr. Lethem growled, as she tried to pry herself from the pole. No such luck. Sable's magical force energy kept Dr. Lethem pinned.

"I will keep your secret for you. Although I have ways to alert Mrs. Chi to your nature—I will not do it if—"

Dr. Lethem's eyes revealed her desperation to have her secret kept.

"I will call on you for a service. You will not hesitate. Or I will tear your world apart. Then you would lose the chance to keep up your charade as the obedient member of Mrs. Chi's crew."

"A service...?"

"I will not ask you to kill Mrs. Chi or a member of the crew—so you can keep that from clouding your thoughts and your days. But keeping your secret will be expensive. It will cost you."

A flash of light—smoke—and Sable Cane had gone.

You turn me into a traitor—just so I have a slim chance to stay with my family—the crew of the Helios. They're all I have, Dr. Lethem thought. Could she go to Mrs. Chi and confess her nature? *No! Once Mrs. Chi knows what I am, she'll know what I did!*

Misery coursed from Dr. Lethem's gut to her heart.

Then she noticed that Sable's magical exit left two streetlamps burned out and some papers on fire in a garbage can on the corner. The flames fluttered, making some shadows dance.

* * * * * *

The flame of a candle reflected on Wrenda's eyes. On board the Helios airship, she sat, resting, in her room. Resting meant that she could recharge from the significant energy she expelled to maintain her *Wrenda-appearance*.

She allowed the artifice of her Wrenda-appearance to melt

away, leaving the visage Marta might recognize, the face of Lord Wu's mother. She had been known as Bing Qing, which meant "clear as ice." Actually, the name fit her well. She'd always had a cold streak in her, the ability to go as cool as ice and not respond immediately in hot anger. Her approach to getting vengeance on the 17-year-old Lihua (later known as Marta Chang) would carry over centuries. Bing Qing had herself turned into a vampire. Then she had centuries to toy with Lihua.

Along the way, Bing Qing—now Wrenda—acquired the magical ability to shapeshift. She had paid for it in multiple ways. She needed time each day to recover, to drop the façade. Still, shapeshifting proved useful.

A vampire and shapeshifter. Unusual. And powerful. Then she augmented her power again: she founded The Council. Marta, of course, knew nothing of this.

Two hundred years ago, Wrenda impacted Marta with The Madness—and then Marta had torn her beloved husband to pieces.

Wrenda watched as Marta had avoided opening her heart for two hundred years.

But Jack AngelSword proved different.

It had almost been a whim that Wrenda had doused Marta with the Orynn water, knocking her nemesis unconscious. So, Jack lived. Marta would have continuing hope that she would enjoy a lifetime—a human's lifetime—with Jack.

The delicious thing for Wrenda: Give a victim hope then snatch away such hope.

Now, Marta and Jack had hope. What would Wrenda do to them next? Wrenda smiled in anticipation.

A knock at her door.

Wrenda did her shapeshifting and bid goodbye to her

Lady Wu face. She regained her visage as Wrenda.

"It's Marta," a voice said at her door.

Wrenda went to her door and opened it.

Marta stood, looking fragile.

"They let you out of the Healing Center?"

"I thought I'd take a walk—almost didn't make it here."

"You could have called me. I'd come down."

"I wanted to talk. To have some privacy," Marta said.

Wrenda felt her concern rise up. She didn't want Marta to collapse. Marta still felt weak after her ordeal with the Madness.

And I had put her through the Madness again, Wrenda thought. *And I ... and I don't feel good about this. This is different. Not like 240 years ago when I had her attack her husband.*

"You're such a good friend," Marta began.

You don't really know me, Wrenda thought.

"These recent years have been better years for me," Marta said. "You've made them better. Thank you."

Wrenda remained silent, listening.

"I didn't become a vampire because I wanted to live long or I wanted to have the strength, the speed ..."

Wrenda nodded.

"It's been ... yes, ten years, and you haven't heard me talk much about the day I had myself turned. When I was 17 years old—"

Wrenda rubbed her forehead with her hand and turned her face down. She couldn't trust her face to not reveal her anguish over her son, Lord Wu.

"I let myself be turned because of my love for Lord Wu."

Wrenda faced away from Marta. Wrenda glanced at the candle that reminded her of a candle that lit the hall so long ago in Ancient China ...

Ancient China. Wrenda—then Lady Wu—heard her son yell, "Be gone from me. You have defiled yourself. You have defiled me! This was not love. This was evil. You have destroyed me."

She then heard a snapping sound. She looked into the royal hall and saw her son, Lord Wu, holding two cylindrical sticks in his hands. He had broken a wooden staff.

Below him, cowering, 17-year-old Lihua (later Marta) still sprawled on the floor. Her face showed her pleading with Lord Wu.

In answer, Lord Wu placed the sharp end of the broken staff facing his chest. He launched himself from the second floor.

The wood pierced his chest and his heart.

Lady Wu cried out.

Her son had released himself from the life of a vampire.

With rage and hatred, she looked at the 17-year-old girl, prostrated on the floor. This girl who had created this tragedy.

Lady Wu withdrew so no one would see her agony. She would bide her time. Her revenge upon the 17-year-old girl would be thorough.

In the present, Marta said, "I was 17. I was wrong."

Wrenda looked at Marta's face.

"I just felt some form of love. But if I was older, if I knew the nuances of love, I would have known to ask him: Did he want his life preserved in the form of a vampire? Did he want to live longer? Did he want to accomplish something? Did want to be with me? Or did he just want to die? I didn't ask him. I didn't give him a choice," Marta whispered.

"What is bringing this up—now?" Wrenda asked.

"I ... I am at another crossroads. And I want to be respectful to you, Wrenda."

"How?"

"I am going to ask to stay on board this airship. To help

with the recovery of Jack AngelSword. And … perhaps, to find out what might Jack's choice be."

"Choice for … oh. Whether he wants to … continue with you," Wrenda said.

"You don't have to stay. I realize that you have other things going on," Marta said.

"I'll stay. For some weeks. It's okay," Wrenda said.

"Thanks. Could I lie down … and rest a while here?"

"Sure."

Chapter 3

Jack AngelSword snarled. Rage and power. That comprised his full experience now. This horrible tornado that he had kept caged—it flowed as his rage in full bloom.

He stood outside Mal Pala's Italian estate ready for the change of the guards. That's when the guards would be off-balance. That's when he would strike.

He was on a mission. His rage had only two desires: full expression and even more power.

After he had been stabbed by the Sword of the Dark Bloom, gone to the Ethereal Plane, shown unspeakable things, he had returned to this world—the Earth. He found himself no longer on the ledge of the St. Mark Campanile.

Somehow, he had been deposited at the bottom of the bell tower.

That was when Jack saw one of his brother Mal's soldiers.

The Cross of Signs pulsated on Jack's right forearm. A vicious leech. Inspiring his rage and feeding on it. He glanced up from the Cross of Sighs and caught a glimpse of that soldier.

Jack leaped forward, reached with his left hand and grabbed the guy by his shirt collar.

"I remember you," Jack said.

"No. I—" Reggie said.

"My brother, Mal, sent an energy bolt at me. I shifted out of the way. The bolt cut one of Mal's soldiers in half and you had a big reaction."

"He was a friend," Reggie said.

Jack's tattoo glowed and then the AngelSword materialized in his in right hand.

Jack held the blade close to Reggie's face.

"Don't you even try lying to me," Jack growled.

"Nick was my—my everything. We were gonna get married. I—" The tears welled up in Reggie's eyes.

"Thought so," Jack said. "Tell me how to take Mal's power from him."

"I—I—"

"Talk quickly or die."

"Mal has an Italian estate. In the safe are sacred text pages. They describe the Judas Gauntlet. Where it has been stored. Where it might be now. How to use it," Reggie said.

Jack nodded. He had seen some details about the Judas Gauntlet in his studies. He kept the information out of his well-received book on comparative religion. The details were mere speculation. And worse, if the Judas Gauntlet truly had its reported power … such power could not be trusted in anyone's hands. Now, with the Rage coursing through his veins, this Overwhelming Power of the Judas Gauntlet taunted Jack as what he most desired.

"You will tell me the estate's location, number of guards, times for the shift changes," Jack said.

Reggie complied.

The Cross of Sighs glowed and *pressed* one idea into Jack's mind: It would be foolish to leave Reggie alive to inform anyone.

Jack shoved the AngelSword through Reggie's chest and through his heart.

You're just the first who will fall to the AngelSword today.

Chapter 4

On board the Helios, Mrs. Chi looked to me. She, Dr. Lethem, Noah, Daniel and I all sat in her Ready Room.

"Jenalee, how long would you keep Trin in the brig?" Mrs. Chi asked me.

"How 'bout eight years?" I said. "Trin, withheld the Silent Scepter and Daniel, and my other friends almost died!"

Daniel nodded.

I glanced at Noah, who nodded. But then I noted that Daniel looked from me to Noah and back again. I could feel it. Trouble was brewing.

Mrs. Chi glanced at Dr. Lethem who continued taking Mrs. Chi's blood pressure.

"I had hoped that you would have taken something from Dr. Lethem's sharing her experience with forgiveness," Mrs. Chi said.

"I did take something. Dr. Lethem, you're a saint. And I am not," I said.

Dr. Lethem smiled.

"Look, I don't know what all this about," Noah began. "But I do know one thing. Mal Pala is still out there. He is not going to stop. And by the way, the last time, he set a werewolf on Jenalee," Noah said.

I saw Noah's concern on his face. It did warm my heart. He was one hundred percent for me—and whatever I would decide. Like when I just said "eight years" for imprisoning

Trin.

"I have agents around the world keeping alert for any trace of Mal," Mrs. Chi said.

"What about where I sent the Chest of the House of Dagger?" I asked. "Is anyone trying to salvage it—from the ocean?"

"Thankfully no," Mrs. Chi said. "But my agents are monitoring the area."

"Good," I said. "But if Mal is not going after the Chest—"

"—then he must have his sights on something else that will get him incredible power," Noah said. "By the way, I, for one, would like to know more about werewolves. Since one tried to kill—"

"Did kill me. That werewolf cut my gut and poured out my intestines," I said.

Noah winced big time.

"Jack used his AngelSword to bring me back to life," I said. As I said this, I remembered how my intestines retreated into my body—under the magical influence of Jack's AngelSword. By the way, I don't recommend anybody having to watch their intestines return into their gut. Ugh.

"Damn! That was vicious," Noah said.

"I have heard that some werewolves take great pains to only kill those who prey on the innocent," Mrs. Chi said.

Dr. Lethem nodded.

"You mean," Noah said. "Some werewolves serve like Draino for the world?

Mrs. Chi smiled. Dr. Lethem, and I joined in with our own smiles. I noted that Daniel didn't smile.

"We still need to capture Mal," I said. "But I think we need to be at full strength. We must get Jack back."

"Jenalee, I do suggest that you consider what an asset Trin can be for your team," Mrs. Chi said.

A knock at the door.

"Enter," Mrs. Chi said.

Ensign Esperanza stepped in. Once again, I noted her enthusiastic energy and willingness to serve the team. "Ma'am. One of our agents reports Jack AngelSword's location."

"Yes?"

"Italy. An Estate belonging to Mal Pala."

"Any estimates of how many of Mal's soldiers are at that site?" Daniel asked.

"Something like twenty," Ensign Esperanza said.

"Thank you for that information," Daniel said.

Ensign Esperanza nodded.

"The Cross of Sighs would make Jack reckless?" I asked.

"I've looked into this. The Cross of Sighs would exacerbate any rage Jack might hold," Mrs. Chi said.

"Jack's going to take on Mal's guards by himself?" I asked, thinking out loud. "This is bad. Real bad."

Chapter 5

Jack watched his hands swing the AngelSword and cut two of Mal's soldiers in half. Blood and guts flying. During the shift change of the estate-guards, the two guys hadn't seen it coming.

The Cross of Sighs had the Rage in Jack in full bloom. Such power. No reservations.

It felt like the world had stepped off Jack's shoulders. Now Jack was free—his Rage was free.

Slice. A diagonal cut. A demon's top half slid down. Then his legs toppled over.

Jack's body whirled in thunderous motion—a decapitated head bouncing off a wall. Two other heads sliced like split-cantaloupes. More bodies fell around Jack.

Jack's body was baptized in blood.

In a corner of his mind, Jack felt horrified. He couldn't stop this. The Rage compelled him forward.

In every other battle, Jack had strived to use the minimum of force. He would even use the AngelSword to cauterize wounds of the opponents who fell before his AngelSword.

Jack saw a guard aim a machine gun at him.

Jack stabbed a close-by guard and used him as a human shield while at the same time some of the bullets were pulled to the AngelSword. This served as confirmation. The AngelSword did act as a magical magnet to bullets. To protect the wielder of the AngelSword.

Soon, his twenty opponents were dismembered heaps all over Mal's Italian estate grounds.

Mal is somewhere else. Fine. I'll look forward to destroying him later, Jack thought. No. It was the Rage in him thinking.

Jack located what must have been Mal's office on the premises. He tore a painting off the wall and found the door to a safe. Using his AngelSword, he burned away the safe's lock.

Jack opened the safe's door, found the pages of sacred text, preserved in something that looked like plastic sheets. He rolled the sheets, grabbed a clip from Mal's desk, clipped the sheets and placed them into his inner pocket—of his overcoat.

Time for a shower. New clothes. Then to study these pages. Massive power felt just a few steps away from him. The Cross of Sighs glowed and still acted like a leech on Jack's right forearm. A snarl of a smile stretched on Jack's face.

"Jack AngelSword is gone, Ma'am," one of Mrs. Chi's agents said over the comm line. "The safe is open. And everyone is dead. All twenty people. Guards and even two maids and perhaps, a butler."

"He's killed non-combatants," Jenalee said. "He's sick. He's possessed, right?"

"In a manner of speaking. I can't know what happened to Jack on the Ethereal Plane," Mrs. Chi said.

"Trin would know," Jenalee said, twisting in her seat in Mrs. Chi's office on board the Helios.

"We must recover, Jack. And now," Jenalee said. Deep concern in her eyes.

"Or we have to stop Jack," Mrs. Chi said, quietly. "To protect more people from him."

Chapter 6

"I've got to get up and find Jack," Marta said, upon opening her eyes. She found herself still on Wrenda's bed on board the Helios.

"Have a good nap?" Wrenda asked.

Marta moved abruptly to sit up, felt dizzy, and lay back upon the pillow.

"You're not fully recovered."

Marta could hear Wrenda's concern in her voice.

A knock at the door.

"Wrenda, is Marta there?" Jenalee Storm's voice.

"Let her in. Maybe she can help me with Mrs. Chi," Marta said.

Wrenda opened the door, and Jenalee stepped in. "Thanks."

Jenalee found a chair and sat down.

"Are you recovered, Marta?"

"I am about—" Marta said.

"She is not. Will Mrs. Chi let us stay aboard while she recovers?" Wrenda said.

"I want to help track down Jack. He needs to be brought in," Marta said.

"That's true," Jenalee said.

"And Marta needs to feed," Wrenda said.

"Oh, yeah. Mrs. Chi's going to like that. Ensign

Tomlinson you made a bad souffle. You're toast. Marta wants to see you," Jenalee said.

"I do not find that funny—" Wrenda said.

"I'm not fully recovered. And it's not safe for me to—"

"Are you at risk?" Jenalee asked. "Are there some Van Helsing heirs tracking you down?"

Wrenda wrinkled her nose in irritation. "There are various clans of vampires and Lycans—"

"Werewolves and vampires really do hate each other?" Jenalee asked.

"A significant number do," Wrenda said.

Jenalee looked straight into Marta eyes.

"Vampire, I don't trust you," Jenalee said.

"Your honesty is refreshing," Marta said.

"Enjoy it. It's raining honesty," Jenalee began. "I don't know what hold you have on Jack—"

"I do not have a hold on him. He just finds me—"

"Don't tell me that the attraction is natural," Jenalee said. "You just carry on your merry way of the predator. Drink up. Who's next? Who's blood do you take! Take! No one is freely giving you—" Jenalee said.

"You don't know why I go for fresh blood," Marta said.

"Don't know. And don't care," Jenalee said.

Wrenda frowned, but Marta smiled.

"Strange," Marta began. "I was given an impression that you are a leader here. Of some sort. Here in the House of AngelSword. Maybe this House is slipping. Over centuries, I've learned that smart leaders listen. They're looking for intel. They're looking for loyalty. You don't have my loyalty yet, sister."

"Sis—?" Jenalee took a deep breath and reminded herself of her keyword "calm." She found that the strain had caused her shoulders to bunch upward. She consciously lowered her shoulders to ease the tension out of them.

"How can any moral human—or creature—," Jenalee said.

"Call me a being. I am one of the Enlightened."

Jenalee had a snappy comeback. She glanced at Wrenda and then back to Marta. Jenalee kept her comeback to herself.

"How can a moral being prey on other beings?" Jenalee said.

"You eat cow flesh, don't you," Marta said.

"Chicken," Jenalee said.

"Lucky cows," Marta said. "Jack respects you. He even told me that you are a good leader. I'll take Jack's impression. For now."

Jenalee remained silent. She put a neutral look on her face.

"I take the blood of fresh donors because I must maintain my top strength," Marta said.

"Why?" Jenalee asked.

"A major war will break out among the Enlightened soon. It is inevitable," Marta said. "My full strength will help me survive."

"What's so special about you?" Jenalee asked.

"That's a whole *other* conversation," Marta said. She focused on Jenalee intently. "Listen close. I am telling you the truth. I would like to know Jack better. I haven't met someone even close to him in over 240 years."

Fifteen minutes later, Marta, Wrenda and Jenalee were gathered in Mrs. Chi's office.

"I'm not sure what to do here," Mrs. Chi said. "Marta, I cannot let you threaten people. I also feel that if I bring you to any particular city, I'm bringing death to that city."

"Perhaps we could come up with some other choice," Marta said. "Often, I notice that this is not a binary world. It seems that you think there is only two choices here."

Mrs. Chi looked at her intently.

"I would like to ask that I stay on board. Or at least that I can accompany the search party that seeks to recover Jack AngelSword," Marta said.

"I am aware that you and Jack have some sort of connection or—"

"Bond. I would like to return the favor. That is, I realize that Jack was an important part of the process—like you were—to have me cured."

Mrs. Chi nodded.

"Perhaps, a third alternative would be to have me rely on some form of blood bank. Maybe through your vast resources, we could purchase enough to sustain me for the next two weeks?"

Mrs. Chi asked what would be the amount of blood that would be enough, and Marta told her.

"Dr. Lethem, I have some things to talk about," Wrenda began as she stood at the doorway to Dr. Lethem's office at the Healing Center.

Dr. Lethem looked up from her computer screen. "Yes?"

"I suggest we close this door, and we speak confidentially. I have been keeping tabs on a number of things," Wrenda said, an edge in her voice.

"Please do shut the door," Dr. Lethem said.

"Doctor, you have not always been as careful as you needed to be. It's come to my attention that you have certain extracurricular activities. Let's say that you tend to sink your teeth into some local resources."

In reaction, Dr. Letham's left hand shook.

"What do you want?" Dr. Letham asked.

"Doctor, I too have a secret," Wrenda said, as she opened her mouth and revealed her incisor teeth elongating. "My secret requires a certain diet. I will require …" And she told Dr. Lethem how much blood bank blood she would need for two weeks.

"Do we have an agreement? I will keep your secret, and you will help me keep my secret," Wrenda said.

Dr. Letham nodded, fervently.

A day later, Wrenda turned to Marta, "How are you doing under this forced blood bank situation?" Wrenda asked.

"Some headaches," Marta said "And I'm not used to having less strength. Apparently, I need to sleep more since my diet has been altered."

"Will you be strong enough?" Wrenda began. "I have a feeling that trying to subdue Jack AngelSword is going to require much strength and much speed."

"I must be. If I'm not fast enough, Jack may be injured or die," Marta said. "I'm not sure how to communicate this. If Jenalee thinks that I'm a liability, she will not grant me permission to join her team."

"When have you waited for permission?"

"When indeed," Marta smiled. "But this is a different situation. These are Jack's people. They are his clan. I—I want to be part of his world."

"You are gone."

"What?"

"You have not only fallen for Jack. You're talking like a starry-eyed teenager."

"Yin and yang," Marta said.

"You sound like you'd like to get hold of his yang."

"Wrenda! A dick joke? This is not your style."

"I'm changing," Wrenda said, simply.

Chapter 7

"Change your approach," Sable Cane said to her new—what? Ally? Yes, Mal Pala had done the spell that released Sable from the InBetween. Sable shivered and did her best to cover her distress as she remembered that dark dimension between realms. She rubbed her hand on her forehead and through her glorious blond hair. Even after the stress of the InBetween, she still retained fashion model-like appearance.

She owed Mal for the action of returning her to the Earth. But as soon as she had discharged the marker, she would move on.

"Doing another assault on the Helios—" Mal continued. Getting worked up, taking big breaths, puffing up his massive chest. He stood nearly seven feet tall, well-muscled and he radiated a powerful masculinity—that did catch Sable's attention.

"There is no need. I have a traitor to Mrs. Chi on board that airship," Sable said, firmly.

"What? So, this traitor can retrieve the Sword of the Dark Bloom—"

"And the Silent Scepter and the Flute of Nightmares for us,"

"How?"

Sable noticed that Mal did glance at her—sometimes in that way. Why not? Blonde and striking in her appearance.

Lithe with feminine grace—but strong.

Then he would focus on something internal, something that drove him.

"I have leverage on her," Sable said.

"Who?"

"I'll keep that quiet for now. The fewer people who know—the less likelihood of something gumming up the works," Sable said.

"Sir," Allen Stilem, Mal's temporary second in command, stood at the door to the office.

Mal looked away from Sable to the doorway, "Make it quick."

"Your brother Jack was seen by two of our agents. The Cross of Sighs in on his right forearm. Jack just killed twenty of our people and took the sacred text from the safe—at your Italian estate."

Mal's body shook with fury that came out of his hand as a bolt of energy that pulverized a chair near Allen Stilem.

Allen made a fast exit from the doorway.

"Take in a breath," Sable said.

Mal did follow her advice. He even sat down in his luxurious chair. Still, his hand tapped on his desk. Betraying his unrest.

"What is the value of the sacred text pages?" Sable asked.

Mal blew out a disgruntled breath. "The sacred text pages will guide Jack to find the Judas Gauntlet," Mal said.

"The final piece of the Obscurum," Sable said.

"You know about that?" Mal asked.

"I know many things. So, we have two levels of information. Are you...concerned with the loss of your people?"

"No. They are tools. My brother, aided by Mrs. Chi's people, is formidable."

"You have my support," Sable said.

Mal glanced at her. He almost said something.

Sable kept a smile on her face. When Mal glanced away she thought, *I'll watch for my chance to use the Obscurum to change reality. I could even change my past. I could eliminate my experience of cancer—and that terrible deal with The Council. To eliminate the threat of The Council to me...the simplest move is to eliminate The Council.*

Mal turned back to Sable and said, "All I care about is that you kill Jenalee Storm. And if you have a spare moment, kill my brother, Jack. Then, my bringing you back from the InBetween is paid for. We'll be square."

"Done," Sable said. "I'll especially enjoy wringing the neck of that Little Girlie."

Chapter 8

I stood at the head of the table. The Ready Room appeared sparse, but somehow warm. In their chairs, Daniel, Noah, Marta, Sahkeisha, Elyse and Mrs. Chi looked at me, expectantly.

"We've been in battle before. Sometimes we've won. Sometimes, we've lost. But this battle is crucial," I said.

"To capture Jack," Sahkeisha said.

"What can we do that twenty guards failed to do?" Daniel asked.

"Be smarter," Elyse Eagle said.

"I like that," I said. "Go further with it."

"Those guards came at Jack straight on. Well, except for the ones that he likely took out by stealth," Elyse said.

"Good point. We avoid the direct approach. 'Hi, Jack. We're here to subdue you. You mind putting your AngelSword away? For old times," Sahkeisha said.

"Mrs. Chi, is there some kind of spell you could give us. Or talisman. Something that can neutralize Jack's AngelSword?" I asked.

"I have been studying this. Checking various sacred texts," Mrs. Chi said. "I'll get back to you on that."

"Shouldn't we have Trin as part of this?" Noah asked. "She's beaten Jack before."

"She's a loose cannon. Let's remember that she stabbed

him with the Sword of the Dark Bloom and that probably made him an easy target for the Cross of Sighs," I said. I glared at Noah.

"Yeah. You got a point," Noah said. "Then, how about Marta here. It seems like Jack is sweet on her. Maybe he'll hesitate with her."

"Besides," Sahkeisha looked at Marta. "You're a vampire. And you're fast. Maybe you could use that talisman on him. Get close. Disable the AngelSword."

I looked at Marta. She still didn't look well.

"Marta is still healing up from the Madness." I began, then I addressed her. "You might not be well enough for the mission."

"I could help—somehow. Maybe distract him," Marta said.

"I'm aware that you and Jack have—an attraction," Mrs. Chi began. "However, from what I'm seeing in my studies that the Cross of Sighs releases any pent-up rage in its victim."

"Damn," Noah said.

"What?" Sahkeisha asked.

"I—I'm thinking that—you know, it's Jack's personal history. I don't like telling tales," Noah said.

"He's got a lot of reason to be angry?" I asked.

"You heard that his mother shot his best friend dead," Noah said. "That's when she killed my brother.... Within hours, Jack got that white streak in his hair."

Jenalee had noticed how the white streak started above Jack's left eyebrow and continued back in his hair."

"He's had it all these years?" I asked.

"It won't go away," Noah said.

"Why aren't you all consumed with rage, too?" I asked.

"It was an accident," Noah said.

I decided to let that detail go.

I wrote on a whiteboard, so everyone could see. "We have a start. Be smarter. No direct assault on Jack. Distract him."

I saw nodding heads.

"Okay. Who wants to add to this?" I said.

Hidden in a recess of an abandoned building, Jack stretched his neck first to the left and then to the right. He could feel it. Another big fight on the horizon. Again, his smile resembled a feral animal snarling.

Nobody better get in my way. I'll cut them down. I'll cut them to pieces.

Chapter 9

"Am I addressing Jack or the Cross of Sighs?" Marta asked. She stood thirty feet away from Jack. She hoped that Jack did not see her condition, not fully recovered from the Madness. And the blood bank fluid failed to give her the nourishment to keep her in top strength and speed.

Jack noticed that her incisor teeth were elongating.

He snorted. "So, you're going to go all vampire on me?"

Like a cornered tiger, Jack moved in a smooth manner—ready to pounce. The abandoned buildings surrounding them served almost like the Roman Coliseum, a place where the best gladiators would meet. Some would win, some would die.

"So, you're still in there, Jack?" Marta asked.

"There is something—someone in the Cross of Sighs. You might say they really have my ear," Jack said.

"From what I saw on surveillance footage, it seemed the Cross of Sighs has your heart imprisoned," Marta said, still twenty feet from Jack.

"No. The Cross of Sighs has released the Beast in me," Jack said.

"Then, you're not the man, I know," Marta said.

In the middle of Marta's sentence, Jack had the AngelSword in his hand and he swung the sword and his body around.

Schissh! The AngelSword destroyed a tranquilizer dart, aimed for the back of Jack's neck.

"Noah," Jack said. "Shooting me in the back. You call that sporting?"

"I call it survival," Noah called out. He immediately moved his position—while maintaining cover. Noah made sure that he would not be in the same place that he had spoken from.

"You might as well all come out. You know I can take you all," Jack said.

"This Cross of Sighs really sucks. It's even giving you a big ego, Jack," Jenalee called out.

Jack turned his attention to his right. Jenalee's voice alerted him to her location. He ran toward her.

Sahkeisha aimed one of her tangle-tree capsules directly at Jack. The AngelSword made quick work of it. But Sahkeisha's other tangle-tree got through and hit the ground.

In an instant, Jack found himself overcome by vines. Almost as quickly, Jack cut himself free using his AngelSword.

Elyse jumped at Jack and soundly hit him on the head with her baton.

Jack spun and did three quick jabs at Elyse with his AngelSword.

The third jab wounded Elyse between her shoulder and neck. She tumbled to the ground.

Sahkeisha gasped and ran over to tend Elyse. She tore off her scarf and used it as she put pressure on Elyse's wound.

With the distraction occupying Jack's attention, Marta moved like the wind and wrapped the Aren Shroud on Jack's left arm. The AngelSword immediately winked out of existence.

"Good night, sweet prince," Marta said and she did a palm strike that knocked Jack unconscious.

"Good work everyone," Jenalee said, stepping from her hiding place.

Sahkeisha looked up from her wounded lover and said, "You call this good work?"

Jenalee swallowed. Her spit tested of bile.

* * * * * *

Sahkeisha watched over Elyse while her dear lover slept. Sahkeisha stared at the bandage on Elyse's neck where but for some grace from above, Elyse had been spared an early death. A flood of anger coursed in Sahkeisha's body, centering in a bile-filled sensation in her gut.

Sahkeisha stepped out of Elyse's Healing Center Room on board the Helios. She searched for Jenalee. With each moment of delay, Sahkeisha grew more agitated until she finally cornered Jenalee in front of Jenalee's room door.

 "Don't you think you should have had a better plan? You think it's okay. Recover one, lose one? On your team?" Sahkeisha said. She shook with fury. "God damn it, Jenalee! You're supposed to lead us. Better than this," Sahkeisha said.

"That's fucking easy for you to say. I didn't ask for this. None of it. I just did what was necessary. Good—I'll quit now!" Jenalee said. "I'm obviously a fuckup at this leadership shit!"

Jenalee slammed the door to her room behind her.

Sahkeisha spun on her heel and strutted past a startled Noah, who had caught the heated exchange.

Thirty minutes went by and then Noah found Jenalee on the SkyLevel and stamping her foot. Jenalee had found no release in a walk among the trees.

Noah took a breath to fortify himself and walked to Jenalee.

"Maybe, it's good," Noah said.

"What the hell could be good?" Jenalee said.

"You've voiced it."

"What?"

"Your real fear."

"That I'm a fuckup?"

"At—?"

"You finish that sentence yourself or I'll break your arm."

Noah just stood there.

"It was my fault. Elyse almost died out there. It wasn't enough that Sahkeisha lost the use of her arm—she lost her life as—"

"A concert pianist."

"Right. And my screwup almost took her—" Tears fell from Jenalee's eyes. "Her everything—her soulmate, Elyse."

Noah opened up his arms. Jenalee fell into his embrace.

Jenalee cried for a time.

When it seemed like she had finished, Noah paused for a moment. "You know what they say about when you meet your soulmate?" he asked.

"What?"

"Run!"

Jenalee pulled back, out of Noah's arms.

"What are you talking about?"

"Run from your soulmate."

"Why?"

"Because your soulmate is going to mess you up! Hit every vulnerable spot. Wake you up."

"You're not saying that Sahkeisha is my soulmate. I don't swing that way."

"That's a relief," Noah whispered.

Jenalee couldn't help herself. She smiled, through the tears.

"Maybe this 'soulmate stuff and run' is sort of like what the Buddha said. I saw a quote that said something like 'If you find fear on your path, go in that direction.' Something like that," Noah said.

Jenalee wiped her eyes. "I saw some other quote ascribed to the Buddha: "Like the moon, come out from behind the clouds! Shine."

"That's it then."

"What?"

"Shine. And no promises that there won't be any clouds," Noah said.

After a few more minutes with Noah, Jenalee felt she needed a break. From everybody. Even Noah.

Maybe especially Noah.

The world felt strange to her now. Things were tilted. Just a few weeks ago, things seemed to be lining up.

She had a boyfriend, Daniel. Was he her boyfriend? They kissed but nothing else.

Was I infatuated? She wondered. Is Noah-and-me real? Is he the one?

She shook her head. And she decided to take a swim in the Helios swimming pool. *I just got to clear my head,* she thought.

In Sahkeisha's room, Sahkeisha held Elyse's hand. "If you leave this planet before I do, I'm going to be pissed."

"Yeah. I love you, too," Elyse said.

Sahkeisha ever so gently hugged her soulmate.

"Ouch!"

"Oh! I'm sorry," Sahkeisha said, jumping back.

"Got ya," Elyse said, just a whisper with a little smile.

Sahkeisha frowned. "This looks like the time for me to tell you a story."

"Oh, good. Storytime."

"My father about two years ago said, 'Sahkeisha, there's something I know is true. Life is a bunch of chapters and life kicks you in the butt into another chapter especially when you're not ready."

Elyse smiled.

Sahkeisha continued, "So my father said, 'Just the last week I was kicked in the butt. You know how your mother is so damn impatient. We're going on our walk. And she's already outside. I know what that means. She basically saying 'hurry up!' So I just discovered that I'm starving. I grab a spoon, open the refrigerator, pull out my leftover bowl of tuna salad and put in two spoonfuls of tuna salad into my mouth. And I rush outside and just as I get to the porch, your mother sees me go bug-eyed. 'Cuz I can't breathe. And I'm feeling horrible pain in my chest."

"'I'm feeling like I'm going to throw up. But I don't want to throw up on the wood paneling of the porch, so I move my body to get to the cement. And I'm thinking, *What a stupid way to die.* My being concerned about making your mother wait and I ate something and then I gave myself a heart attack. What a stupid way to die.'"

Sahkeisha glanced at Elyse like *you're understanding this?*

Elyse held Sahkeisha's gaze.

"My father then said, 'So I sat down on the steps trying to calm myself down. Trying to breathe And eventually my chest stop hurting,'" Sahkeisha continued. "My father looked me straight in the eye and said, 'You know why I am telling this to you?' I replied, 'To show how much you love,

Mom.' My Dad said, 'No. Just because your mother is impatient … Choking on tuna salad is a stupid way to die!'"

Elyse chuckled. Then winced a bit.

"Yeah. Got you. Do you understand why I'm sharing this story with you?" Sahkeisha said.

"So more tuna may live."

"Eeeeelyssse," Sahkeisha said.

"You don't want me to die."

"Right."

Chapter 10

"I'm sad to see you in the cage, Jack," Dr. Letham said.

"These restraints—" Jack began. He glanced around the titanium cage—the same one the Helios crew had used to restrain Marta, only a few days ago.

"Necessary of course. So, you don't have the chance to remove the Aren Shroud from your arm," she said, referring to the magical cloth that prevented Jack from summoning the AngelSword.

"I deserve this. You heard?" Jack said.

"The fight at Mal's Italian estate?"

"It was *not* a fight. It was a massacre. It was as if I was watching my body doing what my heart—my mind would never allow—" Beads of sweat rose on Jack's forehead.

Dr. Lethem took a sudden breath.

Dr. Lethem remembered: Beads of sweat on her own forehead. The window of a subway car had been turned into a mirror, created by the darkness surrounding the subway car. She saw her own face in this makeshift mirror.

This moment, years ago, had occurred after something had bitten her. She barely made it to the subway car. The car doors closed. The subway car raced away, leaving whatever had bitten her far behind.

Thirty minutes later, feeling feverish, she arrived at the door of the Phelps-Linn Hospital, joining others for the night shift. Dr. Lethem had agreed to fill in for another doctor. Duty called. She moped her forehead. She had rounds. She took some rabies shots, fulfilling the protocol for anyone bit by a wild animal.

That night the various patient rooms had an assortment of individuals. It seemed to be a random chance that tonight she would see someone she knew—Dr. Cheng Chi. She smiled, remembering one of their early conversations. Dr. Chi—"call me Charles"—had told her the "Cheng" means "accomplished" so he had grown up with "no pressure." What a pleasant smile he had.

Dr. Lethem had also met Dr. Chi's wife—known to everyone as "Mrs. Chi." His wife seemed a bit formal—still an impressive person.

"Charles, what brings you in?" Dr. Lethem asked. They went through his examination. She ordered some tests. Perhaps, his symptoms only indicated a recent strain of flu.

"Dr. Lethem, you know you're my favorite medical person," Charles began. "No strike that. You're one of my favorite people. What have you been doing? Visiting that boy Bobby Jamison after he—after he—"

"You can say it. Killed my son."

"How can you do it? How can you put aside your anguish?"

"I don't. My anguish. And my compassion live side by side," Dr. Lethem said. "My anguish is—"

That's when she saw the full moon outside the window and her eyes refocused on her right hand transforming into a claw. She brought up her other hand. Now a claw, too.

She glanced at Charles. His eyes. Stark fear.

She felt her chest fill with air. A huge wave of energy. Prey. He is prey. Time to feast. Such delight to tear him apart. Pure feeling. Strength. No fear in me.

Every worry had fallen away.

Nothing left but pure instinct.

She tore his arm off. It was closest.

His screams. Felt natural. The sound of prey.

Just a tiny whisper of horror—some old part of her—the healer deep inside of her—miserable—aghast.

But the rest of her. Completely in this moment. Alive! Strong.

She felt herself smile. Surely it revealed huge teeth.

Her jaws clamped shut on his neck.

His carotid artery spraying blood down her throat. Delicious. Nectar. Better than sugar. A robust taste.

She shook her head like a shark tearing a chunk out of the hide of a baby dolphin.

Charles' neck gave way. His screams silenced forever.

She chewed. Also a delight. Raw meat. The best kind. Fresh.

Just then Mrs. Chi arrived at the doorway. She immediately reached into her purse and pulled out some kind of magical spell-bulb.

Wolf-Dr. Lethem ducked. The bulb caused an explosion that took out the window.

Wolf-Dr. Lethem darted out of the hole that the spell-bulb had created.

Into the night.

As she ran away on all fours. She let out a wild howl.

Again that small whisper of trapped humanity. Still horrified. It wasn't me. Not the me full of compassion and mercy to Bobby Jamison.

No. Just the Beast inside. And that part of her knew that she wanted to tear apart Bobby Jamison.

"Dr. Lethem, how could you understand? All you express is kindness and compassion for your patients here," Jack said.

"I can—" Dr. Lethem began, but then choked on her sentence.

Dr. Lethem could feel the Beast shift inside her.

Perhaps, she could remove the Cross of Sighs from Jack's right arm—to release him from the vicious prison that the Cross of Sighs had created in him. She felt a kinship with Jack.

Dr. Lethem grabbed the Cross of Sighs, pulled hard. The monitors revealed a spike in Jack's breathing, his heartbeat increased. So fast. This thing—the Cross of Sighs—would not let go of Jack. Not without a fight.

Chapter 11

Marta looked up to see Jenalee also arriving at the doorway to the room that held Jack imprisoned in the titanium cage. "Perhaps, you want to go in first?"

"Go ahead," Jenalee said.

Marta entered the room and saw Jack caged and worse— with his arms and legs restrained. Marta's lower lip trembled. Her heart hurt to see Jack reduced to this level.

"I guess turnabout is fair play—" Jack said.

"—now that I'm outside the cage," Marta began. "Don't worry, Jack. I know that Jenalee and Mrs. Chi are all deeply involved with finding some way to free you of that Cross of Sighs."

Jack looked into Marta's eyes. "I don't—I don't know how to carry on with this thing attached to me." He opened the fingers of his left hand. She understood immediately and reached her hand through the bars. She held his hand.

He gave her a little smile. He nodded. "I'm thinking that you understand what I'm going through. I saw you go away into the Madness and struggle your way back," Jack said.

"Back to you," Marta said, giving his hand a squeeze.

Jack glanced at his right forearm with the Cross of Sighs attached like a leech. "This thing has squashed my will." Anguish on his face. Tears came to his eyes.

"What you say is exactly right, Jack. That's what the

Madness did to me," Marta said.

Jack's eyes went glassy, just staring.

"Jack?" Marta gave his hand another squeeze. "Jack!"

Nothing. Jack was gone. His body was alive. But his soul resided elsewhere. Maybe lost in a small corner.

Marta jumped to her feet and darted to the doorway.

She saw Mrs. Chi, with Trin walking at her side, approaching the room where Jack remained imprisoned.

"Help—Jack is—"

Trin rushed past Marta into the room where Jack was imprisoned.

Trin took the chair, reached through the bars and held Jack's hand with both of hers.

"Jack, you remember," Trin began. "'I've seen things you people wouldn't believe.'"

Eyes open, not seeing the room, Jack said nothing.

"Come on, Jack. You know the words. 'I've seen things you people wouldn't believe.'"

Walking in from the doorway, Marta said, "What are you doing?

"It's words from a movie that Jack likes," Trin said.

"What? What movie?" Marta asked.

"*Blade Runner*—made in 1982. I'm trying to jog his long-term memory," Trin said. "Come on Jack. 'I've seen things you people wouldn't—'"

"—believe," Jack whispered.

"Attack ships on—" Trin said.

"—fire off the shoulder of Orion," Jack said.

Trin and Jack said together: "I watched C-beams glitter in the dark near the Tannhäuser Gate. All those moments will be lost in time, like tears in rain."

Trin and Marta had tears in their eyes.

From the doorway, Jenalee saw how both Trin and Marta

were pulling for Jack.

"Time to—" Jack said.

Trin knew that the line in the movie was "Time to die."
She looked in Jack's eyes.

"No, Jack! Stop," Trin interrupted. "Time to *come back to
me*," Trin said, squeezing Jack's hand. "Come back to me,
Jack."

Jack blinked his eyes and looked at Trin. "Trin? It's dark
here. I'm in a dark place."

Jenalee saw something on Marta's face. Marta's deep
concern for Jack and … an awareness that Trin reached Jack
in a certain way.

A way that Marta could not.

Chapter 12

Marta sought out Wrenda. She found Wrenda seated near the large window of the Grand Hall. The clouds like cotton flowing toward the window—toward the Helios.

"How is Jack?" Wrenda asked.

"Bad," Marta said.

Wrenda reached out her hand to comfort Marta. *I'm so mixed up inside,* Wrenda thought.

"Jack was gone. Just his body there. Then … then Trin brought him back," Marta said.

"How?"

Marta explained Trin's successful attempt to bring Jack back by reaching for his long-term memory, of all things, to words from a 1982 feature film, *Blade Runner.*

"I couldn't stay in that room," Marta said. "I thought … I thought Jack and I might be made for each other."

Wrenda blinked at that comment.

Two hundred and forty-three years earlier.

Marta, then known as "Nina," turned to her husband, Ethan Blake, with a twinkle in her eye. "You know you endure my little habits because we're made for each other."

Ethan took her in his arms. With a big smile, he kissed her. They had been married for six months. On his voyage to the Far East, he had met her. Their courtship had been a whirlwind—and joyful.

But they didn't know that a Shadow followed them. That Shadow was Wrenda, who overheard the "made for each other" comment.

No one knew that Wrenda remained near. In the hundreds of years after her son Lord Wu had killed himself, Wrenda had acquired skills and abilities as a shapeshifter. More than that, she had the magical abilities to be that Shadow. Undetectable to even other vampires. Such abilities worked well when Wrenda continued as a hidden stowaway on the ship Marta and Ethan had taken to the American Colonies.

Wrenda, who still thought of herself as Lady Wu, smiled in vengeful anticipation.

She would have her revenge that night—

—when Ethan returned from his meeting which related to how he was privy to the plans of certain colonists to separate from England.

Marta found Ethan to be brave. He only had his mortal life. She had told him the truth of her being a vampire. Ethan told her that he would forego the vampire's existence. Sometimes, in the recent six months, Marta doubted that she could endure it when Ethan would eventually die of old age. And she would be left alone to mourn him.

Wrenda used a vial and poisoned Marta so when Ethan returned he didn't find his loving wife (whom other colonists thought was some type of "Indian"). He found a beast that had succumbed to the Madness.

A prisoner in her own body run by the Madness, Marta watched as her hands literally tore Ethan apart. She would never forget the look of shock and hurt on Ethan's face that began with her tearing his right arm off and continued until he died.

Wrenda, at that moment, drank deep of vengeance.

Wrenda shuddered.

"Are you okay? You're not coming down with

something?" Marta asked Wrenda.

"No. I'm fine."

Marta noticed that Wrenda rubbed her hand over her heart.

"How are you feeling?" Wrenda asked.

"My body is healing. But my heart. You know the pain—it just comes back. It sears me. I—I know this pain. I felt it. When Ethan … when—" Marta could not say, "When I killed him."

Marta finished with "he died." Marta took a breath. "I have not loved anyone since Ethan—"

"Not until Jack," Wrenda said.

Marta nodded.

"And I don't know if I can reach him. Maybe Trin is his match. At least, she is human." Marta's tears fell, and Wrenda embraced her.

Chapter 13

"Really? So you trust Trin now?" I said to Mrs. Chi in her Ready Room on board the Helios.

"Jenalee, to use a phrase—'Can you take it down a notch?'" Mrs. Chi said.

I took a deep breath. I told myself my keyword "calm." It helped. Only a little.

"Fine, I'm … calm," I said. "My point is still valid. Trin actively blocked my efforts and Jack's efforts to get my friends what they needed to keep living." Boom—those last five words had me pissed off again.

"True," Mrs. Chi said.

"So we keep Trin in the brig."

"An important measure of leadership is to know who to forgive, when to forgive and when to start again."

"Pretty words. Always with the pretty words," I said.

"Try these words. 'The test of a first-rate intelligence is the ability to hold two opposed ideas in mind at the same time and still retain the ability to function.'"

"Yeah-yeah. F. Scott Fitzgerald said that."

"No one said your memory has difficulty."

"You're saying that my will—my ego—has difficulty?" I said. Annoyed was a polite word for how I felt.

Mrs. Chi said nothing.

Fine, I thought. *I'll play that game, too.*

I said nothing.

Probably three minutes passed.

Silence.

Mrs. Chi poured a glass of water and handed it to me.

I took the glass and had a drink. It felt good. I didn't want it to feel good. Damn it! I don't like being pushed around by anything—included this friendly neighborhood wise woman.

Fine. "Two opposed ideas in mind at the same time." Trin is a traitor. Trin's stubbornness almost cost me the lives of my friends. Why couldn't we have shared the Silent Scepter? Taken turns with it?

I got up.

I bowed to Mrs. Chi and quietly left her Ready Room.

* * * * * *

In his office at his Mexican estate, Mal turned and faced Sable Cane. He pulled none of his intensity down. "Now is the time for us to recover the Sword of the Dark Bloom, the Silent Scepter and the Flute of Nightmares," he began. "I still say the efficient way is to make another attack on the Helios."

Sable turned to her harpy assistant, Hellene. Sitting on the corner of Mal's desk, Hellene flapped her wings. She knew her sitting on his desk irritated Mal. That was why she did it.

"Typical. He's lost in a fog of testosterone," Sable said.

"Certainly. See how his nose scrunches up in a feral grimace," Hellene said.

"Enough! I'd say, 'Look at the two harpies chirping away.' But that is too obvious," Mal said.

"Subtlety, thy name is not Mal Pala," Hellene said, smiling.

Mal raised his right hand, just about toss a bolt of energy at Hellene.

"Mal—" Sable said, in a tone that sounded like a purr.

It stopped Mal in his tracks.

"I've already given the assignment to my traitor aboard Mrs. Chi's Helios," Sable said. "Perhaps, in as little as two days, you'll have the artifacts—the three parts of the Obscurum."

"Jack AngelSword was last seen by my agents with the Cross of Sighs fused with his right arm," Mal said. "The AngelSword plus the Cross of Sighs will make him more powerful than ever before. We already know that he plowed through twenty of my people on my Italian estate."

"Strategy, Mal. We have strategy," Sable said. "You'll have the combined power of the three artifacts. So, he'll have the Cross of Sighs still on his arm. We'll just cut off his arm,"

"That will work," Mal said. His turn to smile.

* * * * * *

In another dark corner of the world, VoSkhar turned to his top assistant and confidant Zara, who lounged around in her jaguar form.

"You've been keeping your guise as Master Haito rather low-key recently. Why?" jaguar-Zara asked.

"I feel it," VoSkhar smiled. An enigmatic smile known to the world as his trademark on magazines and the top blogs, in his role as a master entrepreneur with hundreds of companies.

Beings, including vampires, Lycans and others of the mystical world, knew VoSkhar as the leader of the House of Dagger.

Jaguar-Zara watched as VoSkhar's form changed. His ear

tips sharpened and elongated. His smile became grotesque—big, spiked teeth. Now, VoSkhar stood in his foundational and real form—the demon Khodan.

"Feel what, exactly?" jaguar-Zara asked.

"The energy is shifting. We must watch closely. Since the anointing of Jack AngelSword as the Sword of Balance—everything has sped up. His brother Mal Pala has intensified his efforts."

Snap!—jaguar-Zara broke the top of a nearby chair with her claws.

"I will snap Jack AngelSword's neck!" she growled. "Just like he cut my brother down."

"Of course. You will avenge Erik. But look for a sign from me, Zara," Khodan-VoSkhar said. "Every action must be strategic."

Jaguar-Zara said nothing. She shook with rage. Death was coming for Jack.

Chapter 14

When Jenalee got to her feet and left Mrs. Chi's Ready Room, she felt on a mission.

Sure, Mrs. Chi's tactic of silence and then giving Jenalee a glass of water had worked in some way. Jenalee had a new idea.

She went to the brig. No Trin. Of course. Jenalee knew the one place for Trin to be.

With her hands reaching through the bars of the titanium cage, Trin held Jack's hand.

Sometimes, Jack would drift away, and she would bring him back by getting him to recite the words from *Blade Runner*.

"I've seen things—

"You people wouldn't believe." Trin and Jack said, together.

"Jack, what did you see on the Ethereal Plane?"

With his eyes clear, Jack peered directly into Trin's eyes. "What did *you* see?"

"For a moment, I saw you—" Trin began. "And—it looked like Uncle Richard in spirit form."

"You're fucking right! What he showed me—I couldn't—I couldn't escape it. Did you see that horror?" Jack asked.

Trin reached her right hand to Jack's shoulder. "I didn't—

I was pulled away. I saw something else."

Jack shuddered. "It was like an acid waterfall. Burning. Images. Every time I was angry. Every time I lashed out—angry, cutting words. Hurting my mother with words. Words punishing her for killing my best friend, Mark. My rage. At my father—his throwing me into walls, spitting on me—when my mother was out of the house." The words pouring out of Jack like a bitter vomit.

"My father hitting my mother. Until... when she learned to defend herself at the Police Academy. The one time she defended herself and did a sword hand strike to his throat. Taking him down. That moment. That's when he stopped letting his rage pour onto her. She could take him. The bully was stopped, gasping for air, all 250 pounds of him on the floor," Jack said.

Jack's fists started closing. Trin barely extricated her left hand.

"My disgust and rage at my own father boiled."

Trin watched concerned. Then out of her peripheral vision, she noted Jenalee's presence at the doorway.

"My rage—my disgust—my moral outrage—You're my father. You're my mother's husband! God DAMN you!" Jack shook. He struggled against his restraints. Suddenly, his eyes went glassy.

"Jack!"

Jenalee stepped close. "Call him back. Bring him back."

"Jack. Come back. Say it, 'I've seen things you people wouldn't believe.'"

Jack's vacant stare remained.

Trin tried five more times to jog Jack's long-term memory—to pull him back.

Tears in her eyes, Trin slouched back in her chair. "I've been with him for hours."

Jenalee listened intently.

"He comes in and out. But then I had an idea on how to release him from the grip of the Cross of Sighs."

"Yes?"

"We take him to Master Haito. My guide in the mystical arts. He'd know what to do," Trin said.

"You sure about this?" Jenalee said.

"Yes. Master Haito helped me. I was ... I was in despair over the death of my father. Master Haito could sense that. He helped me. I trust him. The question is ..."

"... will I trust you," Jenalee said. "I was talking with your mother."

"That's always a journey," Trin said.

Jenalee smiled despite her misgivings.

"I have a question for you," Jenalee said. "Why would you not share the Silent Scepter?"

Trin breathed deeply, bracing herself.

"My mother. She has tunnel vision. It is always the mission. Casualties? It's the cost of war. Once my mother got her hands the Silent Scepter, it was likely she would not release it. Then, my own friends—Curry and Kyle—they are my family ... My mother would let my own family die—to serve *her* own noble cause."

"Then you don't trust your own mother," Jenalee said.

"That was true at that time. That was before I went to the Ethereal Plane," Trin said. "I don't have the words yet. I came to know. Know it in my heart...some things."

"Some things people wouldn't believe?" Jenalee said, quoting the words from *Blade Runner*.

Trin smiled. "You might say that."

"There is something I know. You have always gone easy on Jack," Jenalee said.

"That is true. I ... I care about Jack."

"It's more than that."

"… yes. It's more than that," Trin admitted.

Jenalee stood taller, shifting her shoulders back.

"Then, it's settled. I will trust you to protect, Jack. You and I will take Jack to Master Haito."

Trin smiled. "I … thank you."

Just before her departure with Trin—to take Jack to Master Haito—Jenalee had a vital idea. She explained it to Mrs. Chi who helped her implement it.

Twenty minutes after they had prepared and completed a particular magical spell, Jenalee asked Mrs. Chi, "Will this work?"

"Uncertain. But your intention was good," Mrs. Chi said.

"My idea arose on hearing Trin speak of the Ethereal Plane," Jenalee said. "The White Dragon is searching for his mate. I just realized what dimension might be most promising."

Jenalee had basically sent a magical "message in a bottle" out to the White Dragon. In her message, she said, "White Dragon. This is Jenalee Storm. I had a thought. The most likely prison that the Crimson Dragon sent your mate to would be in a dimension that is *most* inhospitable to dragons. He'd want her to suffer. And you to suffer. Focus your search on such terrible places. Even places where she might die immediately. I had the intuitive image of her being in something like a 'bottle' of energy. White Dragon, thank you again for your kindness to me. May this message serve you and reunite you with your soulmate. Jenalee Storm out."

Jenalee thought, *A message in a bottle cast out across dimensions. Even, possibly to the Ethereal Plane. Maybe the message would reach the White Dragon.*

Some things are worth trying even with the slimmest chance.

Chapter 15

"Master Haito asks that no more than two people accompany, Jack," Trin said to Jenalee as they discussed final preparations in Mrs. Chi's Ready Room aboard the Helios. Trin still felt relief that she was able to get a message, finally, to Master Haito after over 60 of Mrs. Chi's agents put out the word.

"Why?" Jenalee asked.

"I don't know. He has been my teacher," Trin said. "He always has a good reason. Who knows. Maybe, when he frees Jack of the Cross of Sighs, there would be problems with there being too many conflicting energies in the room."

"What do you mean conflicting?"

"I know from my magic-studies with Master Haito that … that people all have different rhythms. It's how some people just click with each other when they meet—"

"Like you and Jack?" Jenalee asked.

"Well—we—we got along," Trin said. "I mean, if we didn't have opposing agendas at the time."

"Right. Jack was just trying to save my friends in a coma—

"Could we just—just put that aside for now? I'm right here now. We want the same thing—to save Jack."

"Thank you, Master Haito," Trin said as she sat back in a chair at a martial arts studio Master Haito borrowed for this occasion.

Trin looked at her teacher. The master of martial arts and mystical arts smiled. A great smile. He looked so at peace. So calm. She felt safe.

Trin glanced at Jenalee. Not much trust there. Jenalee looked wary. Jack rested, plopped in a chair. His arms and legs were shackled in a special way. Jack has no way to use his right hand to take off the Aren Shroud that deactivated his AngelSword. With his hands behind him, he could not even remove the Aren Shroud with his teeth.

Master Haito looked at Trin. Lithe, attractive. Her almond eyes revealing her trust. It was good to see her again.

Trin didn't know that Master Haito comprised merely a guise that demon Khodan used. Just another "suit" like *VoSkhar* that Khodan used.

Wouldn't Trin be surprised if she somehow found out that her mentor was none other than VoSkhar, the leader of the House of Dagger—sworn enemy of Mrs. Chi of the House of AngelSword? Khodan-VoSkhar thought.

"It was wise to bring him here," Master Haito said. "You must have done a lot of work to find me."

"I had help," Trin said. She hadn't seen Master Haito in two years—since the time her heart had broken.

After a significant time of training Trin ... Master Haito said,. "I must step away. Do not worry. I have no trouble. I'm just needed somewhere else. Other people need me."

"Can we stay in contact via Facebook—email—something?" Trin asked. Her eyes revealed her distress to be losing Master Haito's support.

"You don't need me. This is the completion of a chapter of your

life."

Tears came to Trin's eyes. "Another important person leaves my life."

"People come, and they go. A chapter closes—a chapter opens."
Master Haito said gently.

"Your leaving will be another brick for me to carry around,"
Trin said.

He hugged her.

Then he was gone.

But now, Trin felt Master Haito's calming presence back in her life. She felt deeply grateful that Mrs. Chi had set her agents to work to track down Master Haito.

Trin's heart had filled with joy when she learned that Master Haito would grant her an audience.

Jenalee glanced at Master Haito and at the surrounding room. Something felt off. She didn't know what it was, but she could feel the tension in her neck just above her trapezius muscles. Peering at Trin, Jenalee tried to assess whether she could somehow surreptitiously inform Trin that something was off. No help there. Trina appeared enthralled to be in the presence of Master Haito.

I wish Sahkeisha was here, Jenalee thought. But Sahkeisha had chosen to stay with Elyse in the Healing Center—on board the Helios.

Master Haito looked into Jack's eyes which were still glassy.

Master Haito's hands began to glow and he placed them on Jack's shoulders.

What is going on? Jenalee asked herself. *Why do I feel so on edge? Maybe somebody's watching—*

Just then Zara, in her jaguar form, burst from a door

hidden in a wall. She grabbed Jack and threw him into another wall. Jaguar-Zara growled, *"You killed my brother. I don't care if you were protecting the girl. A life for a life,"* It was clear that she was going to kill Jack on the spot.

Crashing through the rice paper door, Marta managed to knock jaguar-Zara aside just enough so that her claw missed Jack's neck and only sliced his shoulder.

Marta kicked jaguar-Zara with such force that she slammed into Master Haito who struck a wooden cabinet. On striking his head, Master Haito shimmered—his form flickering between the images of Master Haito, VoSkhar and his true form, the demon Khodan.

Dazed, the demon Khodan-VoSkhar blinked his eyes while struggling to regain his composure.

"This revelation is premature. No matter. Time for you to die," Khodan-VoSkhar said. Then he returned to the form of VoSkhar. He spoke into a microphone embedded in his sleeve.

"Attack now."

In a blur, Jenalee pulled her fighting sticks from her quick-release holsters, secreted below her jacket.

Nine of Khodan-VoSkhar's soldiers entered.

One fired his gun and caught Marta in the gut with a round. Jaguar-Zara took advantage of the moment to slash Marta, tearing up her right side and then her back.

With her fighting sticks, Jenalee took out the gunman and two of his buddies. Marta fell down below the onslaught of jaguar-Zara's strikes.

A thought flashed in Jenalee's mind. Marta's weak on blood bank blood and the Madness has disabled her. Jenalee kicked a soldier so he collided with jaguar-Zara.

In her bloodlust rage, jaguar-Zara sunk her claws into the soldier and tossed him aside.

We're outnumbered. We're going to lose, Jenalee thought. Still, she fought on with her fighting sticks.

Explosions took out two of the assailants and punched jaguar-Zara back against a wall.

The source of the weapons-fire were two drones operated by Daniel.

Jenalee swung to hit a soldier. Thud! The Helios elevator car smashed through the roof to land on this soldier. That was convenient.

Two of Mrs. Chi's soldiers jumped out the elevator can and helped Trin and Jenalee pull Jack and Marta into the elevator car.

The elevator car rose quickly. A last-minute save.

Struggling to catch her breath, Jenalee felt grateful. But that didn't stop her from glaring at Trin.

Trin still appeared shocked that her beloved mentor turned out to be both demon Khodan and the head of the House of Dagger.

Jenalee knew that Trin had a thing for Jack. But this whole Master Haito thing was one fucking, bad mistake.

Chapter 16

On board the Helios, crew members carried Jack and Marta to the Healing Center.

Exhausted, Jenalee nodded to Daniel, who operated his drones to enter a side docking station.

Daniel looked back to Jenalee, already about nine feet away.

"Got to lie down. I gotta rest," Jenalee called back.

"Sure. Uh, see you later," Daniel said.

The next morning, Jack still slept. Trin slept in the room, just outside the titanium bars of the cage. Trin had arranged some chairs as her makeshift bed.

Marta remained in another room of the Healing Center, recovering from her wounds sustained in her brief battle with jaguar-Zara.

Trin opened her eyes, felt the familiar urge and left to use the restroom.

A moment later, Noah stepped into the room. His neck muscles tensed upon seeing his friend back in the titanium cage.

"We got to get you outta here, buddy," Noah said.

". . . I agree," Jack said, blinking his eyes and waking up.

"Jack? You in there?"

"In this cage. Kind of obvious, right?"

"No. I mean. Look, you were winking in and out of being

conscious over the recent two days," Noah said.

"Right. It's been a blur. Trin has been here," Jack said.

"Yes. We've all visited."

"Marta? I have a vague—I guess, memory. Marta saved me from a big cat. How the hell did that happen?"

"She saved you from a shapeshifter."

Jack blinked. *"You killed my brother. I don't care if you were protecting the girl. A life for a life,"* Jack remembered.

"I remember," Jack said. "The jaguar-somebody. I think I killed her brother … when he was in werewolf form."

"Some kind of life we're having—" Noah said with a bit of a smile.

"No kidding."

Jack took a breath and glanced at the Aren Shroud on his arm. He realized the Shrouds purpose: "I see that my AngelSword has been neutralized."

"Okay. I'll give you some other weapon," Noah said.

"What?"

"We'll stick some Tic Tacs up your butt and when you fart, you can use them as projectiles."

"Come here, Mal, I got something for ya."

Jack and Noah laughed. For just a moment, they were just two friends feeling okay.

Jack looked at his best friend. "Are you still reading that John Carter Likes Bars?"

"Of Mars, you idiot!"

They laughed again.

"Jack?" Noah sat down on a seat, outside the titanium cage. "Are you in pain?"

"No."

"Good to hear."

"Are your thoughts swirling around?" Noah asked.

"Not at the moment. It's actually a relief," Jack said.

Noah sat back in his chair. *Jack is okay in this moment,* Noah thought.

Jack saw something on Noah's face and asked, "Something going on?"

"Jack, you got to help me!"

"Help you what?"

"Defeat this Daniel-guy."

"What? Oh—you mean, your rival for Jenalee's affection," Jack said. Jack welcomed this moment in which he could be supportive of his friend.

"This Daniel-guy is pulling out all the stops," Noah said.

"How?" Jack said.

"First he's all vulnerable. Getting over that magic-augmented virus. Jenalee feels sorry for him." Noah began. "Then he's all brave—as he does his rehabilitation exercises. Watch him struggle. It's all with that 'No, let me do it by myself.' How do I compete with that?"

"Don't compete," Jack said.

"What? Forget that. I found out that he did that three desserts thing with Jenalee—some weeks ago. Before I even met her."

"I've noticed. People who are meant to be together will be together," Jack said.

"Aaaah. Who am I talking to? How about your taste in women? One wants to bite you—not in a good way," Noah said.

"What's a good way?" Jack asked.

"You know love bites. What? You've never had a hickey?" Noah said. "God! You led a sheltered life."

* * * * * *

Daniel and Jenalee entered the Grand Hall, just as Noah

exited a side door. Daniel saw Noah, but Jenalee missed seeing him.

"So what's his story?" Daniel asked Jenalee.

"What?" Jenalee asked.

"Noah. What's his story?"

"He shoots people dead."

"What?"

"It's for a good cause."

"Save the whales is a good cause," Daniel said. "What?—he can't wound people? You know, shoot them in the leg or arm?"

Jenalee rolled her eyes skyward, and she thought. *Oh God. This thing again.* "I'll boil it down to a sentence or two. Noah says if he clears his holster, then he's made a decision that the threat is deadly. It's like how police officers are trained, okay?"

"He's a police officer?"

"He's like a soldier—for Mrs. Chi."

"All right. That makes sense."

"Does everything have to make sense?" Jenalee said, her voice loud and sharp. "You know, there are some things that are beyond science?!"

Concerned, Daniel looked at Jenalee. "What's bringing this on?"

"I … I don't know. I need to take a walk," Jenalee said.

"I'll go with you," Daniel said with a smile. But he saw the frown on Jenalee's face. "Oh, you want some quiet time."

Jenalee nodded. She stepped away. She disappeared as the elevator door closed behind her.

Daniel thought, *What did I do? I just got wounded. And this Noah-guy looks like he's moved in.*

Jenalee's thoughts and feelings whirled like a tornado

inside her. She went to the SkyLevel for some relief. Trees and the open window area, letting the fresh air in.

It was no use. She didn't feel better. She didn't feel calm. *Why the hell did I snap at Daniel? He didn't do anything wrong. I'm the one who's fucked up. I believed Trin. And it turned out she had been major-time fooled by a demon! Master Haito—Trin's teacher—was a damn demon!*

Noah stepped out of the elevator—about thirty feet behind Jenalee.

He saw her and walked up.

Jenalee turned and said, sharply, "What? Can't anybody give me some space?"

"Whoa!" Noah said. "I was going to ask if you thought—"

"I'm not thinking. I'm here to chill," Jenalee said.

Noah started to retreat.

"I'll wear a bell next time, give you some warning," Noah said.

"Is that supposed to be funny?"

"I was—I'll just catch you another time," Noah said and spun on his heel, stepped to the elevator, and left Jenalee alone.

Being alone, to Jenalee, did *not* feel better.

Daniel walked to the door of the room that Sahkeisha and Elyse shared.

He knocked, and Sahkeisha opened the door.

"Can you help me out?" Daniel asked.

"Sure. Which way did you come in?"

Daniel looked at her like she was strange.

"There went my career as a stand-up comedian," Sahkeisha said.

Daniel looked serious and concerned.

With compassion in her voice, Sahkeisha said, "Daniel,

are you okay?"

"I don't know. Is Jenalee okay?" Daniel said.

"What do you mean? Is she sick?"

"You tell me—what's going on with this Noah-guy?" Daniel asked.

"Oh no, I'm *not* getting in the middle of this one," Sahkeisha said.

"So, there's a middle."

"Dammit. I didn't want to get into this."

"Too late," Daniel said.

Sahkeisha smiled a bit and stepped out and closed the door. "Elyse is resting right now."

Daniel and Sahkeisha said nothing for a couple of moments.

Then he slammed his fist on the door frame. "Owww!"

"Well, that wasn't smart," Sahkeisha said.

"I can't compete with him. He shoots people."

"Only ones that deserve it,"

Daniel turned and looked at her.

"So, don't deserve it."

"Seriously, I don't know what to do," Daniel said.

"Then don't compete, just be real. Just be there for her. And if it's supposed to be, it'll be," Sahkeisha said.

"Oh great. You just gave me a fortune cookie fortune."

"Some things are true, and they do not need a lot of words," Sahkeisha began. "In high school, I had to read something by a guy, a philosopher, named Immanuel Kant. All I can tell you is he *kant* write."

"Yeah… He had good ideas. He said 'Science is organized knowledge. Wisdom is organized life.'"

"That sounds pretty. Where was that sentence in the book that I had to read for my psychology class?" Sahkeisha said.

"Come on, Sahkeisha. Who are you rooting for?" Daniel

said.

"What?"

"Noah or me?"

"Jenalee!" Sahkeisha said.

"That's a cop-out."

"I'm not getting into the middle of this. Besides, how would I know? I don't swing hetero, anyway. Ya ain't anywhere near my type," Sahkeisha said.

Elyse opened the door and said, "And good thing, too. Or I'd have to take my baton to your nuts."

Daniel grimaced.

"Yeah. Yeah. No help here," Daniel said.

"I got one piece of advice." Sahkeisha shifted to a spooky voice: "Beware of the Friend Zone! Oooooooo!"

"Everybody's a comedian," Daniel said.

Sahkeisha said, "Damn straight. I mean, damn right."

Jenalee ate a snack in the Grand Hall. Sahkeisha stood at the soft-serve—ice cream machine.

"Could have used your help out there," Jenalee said, from her table.

"Really? You want to pick up our conversation that way—and here?" Sahkeisha said.

"All right. All right. Chill. I supported the idea of you staying with Elyse. I didn't push you, right?"

Sahkeisha paused.

"I miss Magic," Sahkeisha said.

"What?"

"I miss Magic—in his cat form. You could pine away for his bad-boy appearance if you—"

"I don't—"

Sahkeisha sat down at the table with Jenalee. "Really? I saw you go all hetero-girl a-flutter around him."

"That's just—" Jenalee went silent.

"You know that last thing you said around me is that you want to quit. Evidently, you didn't quit."

"Evidently," Jenalee said. "Still want to, though."

"I still miss Magic. Hey, I don't see any animals on board the Helios. Do you know how Magic is doing?

"Two days ago, I talked with the neighbor, Ms. Ahlei. She's still delighted to have Magic at her home."

"I'm sure that Magic is keeping to his cat form around the neighbor," Sahkeisha said.

"He's smart."

"I miss … you," Sahkeisha said and reached out to Jenalee.

The best friends hugged.

* * * * * *

About fifteen minutes later, Jenalee rested back at her cabin. Magic's face, in his gorgeous human form, came back to her mind. Again.

He had looked so upset when he had heard that she had been attacked by the werewolf.

It seemed like Magic wanted to say something to her. Maybe to give her some excuse for why he had just strayed away.

What could he say that would make up for his abandoning her? True—she hadn't been under attack when he had stepped away … but still, this bothered her.

She made sure that he had someplace to be with Ms. Ahlei. And he was probably stuck in his housecat form since he had given his personal energy to help heal Gram-Gram.

Jenalee winced. The pain of Gram-Gram's absence hit her in the gut and in the heart.

Magic, in his housecat form, winced. He felt bad. He just continued to rest with his head on his paws in Ms. Ahlei's garage. He didn't have the energy to be around even a kind human like Ms. Ahlei.

I'm probably still feeling bad about leaving Jenalee—and minutes later she was attacked by a werewolf. If I had been there, I could have done something to help her. Damn!

He stood up, swooshed around and knocked an old, nearly-empty paint can off a shelf with his tail.

How am I going to get Jenalee to forgive me? If I just tell her what happened, will that be enough? He saw his own shadow, created by the sun coming through the window of the Ms. Ahlei's garage. His shadow reminded him:

Magic saw his own image reflect in a shop window. This was days ago—when Magic walked with Jenalee during their errand to get groceries. He continued to glance around. Things looked different. Standing in his human form gave him a whole different perspective. He felt a stab of pain in his chest.

What? I'm being called ….

It's Aunt Fiona. She is twelling. She's calling me—she's hurt. Someone's attacked. She could die.

I must run to her!

Magic ran in his human form.

No—I can run faster as a cat.

He ran behind a dumpster and changed form.

As I cat, he ducked around humans' legs and past cars.

Hang on, Fiona! I'll be there soon. *He twelled back to her.*

When he arrived in Golden Gate Park, he found four youths—15 or 16 years old—throwing rocks at Aunt Fiona who was bloody and in her bobcat form.

She must be weakened, and she can't change to a human

form.

Rage. With his claws, Magic jumped and disarmed the youths, giving them severe wounds as he slashed them. Souvenirs for when they tried to kill a bobcat. Not a bobcat, my own family member—a Feyleene—you, assholes.

The youths bled from significant wounds—they all needed stitches. Two of them cried and called for help with their cell phones.

You're not going to die. But you're paying for what you did. At least a little.

With the youths occupied, Magic went to Aunt Fiona. He turned to human form and pulled a vial from the gold chain he wore around his neck. He helped Aunt Fiona have a drink.

The magical elixir would sustain her and enhance her healing. She would be okay.

Magic shook his head in his cat way of relieving tension. I still feel bad about leaving Jenalee alone. *Am I ever going to get her to forgive me? I could go to Gram-Gram. Maybe, she could give me some ideas. But she's gone again—I guess on some kind of mission.*

Magic had no idea that he'd never see his dearest friend Gram-Gram ever again.

* * * * * *

Dr. Lethem's right hand shook as she used her left hand to put medical supplies on the top shelf of her office. She had been given her order from Sable Cane: Deliver the Silent Scepter, the Flute of Nightmares and the Sword of the Dark Bloom.

For five years, Dr. Lethem had been a trusted member of Mrs. Chi's Helios crew. More—it was like Dr. Lethem was part of Mrs. Chi's family. All of this would come crashing down, if Sable Cane alerted Mrs. Chi to how Dr. Lethem had killed Mrs. Chi's husband. No relationship could survive that.

Dr. Lethem still carried the relief that on the night that she had killed Mrs. Chi's husband and escaped out the window, that she had a cover story. An inmate got loose and when Dr. Lethem came back to the hospital, she was kept outside because the facility was on lockdown. Dr. Lethem explained that she had taken a break and had been on a walk outside the hospital.

With both her own son and Bobby dead, Dr. Lethem had no one outside the Helios. She had no place other than the Helios to be. The Helios was her home. She would do anything to keep her home and her Helios family.

She would deliver the artifacts.

Sable Cane had said nothing about the Cross of Sighs. Dr. Lethem had overheard that the Cross of Sighs was part of a set that included the other three artifacts. The name of the set—The Obscurum.

Dr. Lethem would take a chance. She would *not* report to Sable Cane that the Cross of Sighs was on board the Helios. If Sable Cane heard that the Cross of Sighs remained fused to Jack AngelSword's arm, the heinous woman would probably want Dr. Lethem to amputate Jack's arm.

No! I won't do that! I'm a doctor. I will do no harm. There has to be a line that I will not cross, Dr. Lethem told herself.

But was that true?

Chapter 17

"What's next?" Wrenda asked Marta—who remained, recovering in the Healing Center. In the private room, they could talk freely.

"I'm sure that Jenalee and Mrs. Chi are looking at every possibility."

"Not Trin?"

"It was Trin's plan that failed spectacularly."

Wrenda added a pillow under Marta's head and shoulders to make Marta more comfortable.

"Can you get a laptop ... I mean, I think they have these hPads—your know, the small computers and—"

"Yes. Will you be resting first?" Wrenda said. She lit a candle.

Flickering flames—12 years ago. the horrible image during a news broadcast caught Wrenda's eyes. a small plane had crashed and caught fire. No survivors. Soon she learned that the man and woman who had died in the plane crash were her dear friends Alexander and Miranda.

At the moment Wrenda saw the news report her heart felt crushed like a car in a compactor.

She knew. And, she stood in the kitchen making dinner for Alexander and Miranda's daughter Susannah. For six years, she had been Suzannah's godmother. She had been in the room holding Miranda's hand at the moment of Suzannah's birth.

From the moment, Susannah could talk she made it clear that she couldn't stand pink. She preferred blue. A blue dress was okay. A pink dress was "garbage."

Susannah and Wrenda would often playfully talk about how Wrenda could act like Susannah's fairy godmother. They even went to a toy store and found a little wand so that when they played, Wrenda would wield the little magic wand and say, "Make the way smooth and joyful for this little girl." On this day of the plane crash, those days felt long gone.

As Wrenda watched the TV news footage of the burning plane on the ground, she knew that she faced having to say something to Susannah that was going to burn her world down to the ground.

"Susannah," Wrenda called out.

"I'm coming!" Susannah called out in her clear, cheerful voice. She ran into the kitchen.

"You going to wave your magic wand over our lunch, Wrenda?"

"I ... I need you to sit down."

"Something wrong?"

"It is something that—" Wrenda began.

Susannah looked over Wrenda's shoulder at the burning plane on the TV.

"Is that Daddy's plane? Are—are daddy and mommy dead?"

This caught Wrenda by surprise.

"They—they are dead." It felt all wrong to tell a six-year-old girl such a harsh thing. But trying to dress this tragedy up in euphemisms felt wrong, too.

Susannah's usual fast-paced talking was snuffed out at that moment. In fact, she never chittered as a fast-paced talker again. She just sat there. Looking at the TV. Tears pouring down her face.

Quietly, Susannah asked, "Where will I live?"

"You'll live with me," Wrenda said. "I'll take care of it. Remember, I'm your godmother."

"God. Why did God take away my parents?" Susannah asked.

Wrenda saw her right-hand shaking. Tears flowed down Wrenda's face. "Susannah, I don't know. But I'm certain about something. I want you to know I love you, and you're going to be okay."

"You okay, Wrenda?" Marta asked.

"—yes, okay. I was … remembering Susannah—when she heard about her parents' death," Wrenda said.

"You want to talk about it?"

"No. Not at the moment. Over these years, you've heard about it plenty."

Wrenda pulled out a brooch from her pocket.

"You still have it," Marta said.

The brooch in her hands. Ten years ago. This day had been ghastly so far.

Every half-hour or so, the wave of grief would hit Wrenda. Such emotional pain—she'd have to sit down.

Three hours ago, that's where Marta had found Wrenda. This was the first time Marta had laid her eyes on Wrenda (actually Lady Wu in her 'Wrenda-form').

Normally, one vampire could recognize another vampire, but Wrenda had perfected her spells. Wrenda had become a vampire, proficient in shapeshifting and cloaking herself so other members of the Enlightened would not know Wrenda's true nature.

Wrenda sat on a bench in the upscale shopping mall. She couldn't get herself to enter the store.

To go into the store was again to solidify that little Susannah, just eight-years-old, was dead. There was no good reason for her to be dead.

In the hospital, Susannah lay dying of an infectious disease. She asked Wrenda, "Why didn't Joey's parents get him vaccinated?"

"Probably they were scared," Wrenda said.

"Scared?"

"They probably didn't trust that the vaccination would be safe."

"They were scared. I'm so cold. I'm scared. Am I going to die?

Wrenda held her. "I'm right here. I'll talk to the doctor. We'll take care you."

"Yeah, you always take care of me," Susannah said.

Sitting on the bench in front of the clothing store, Wrenda could not take care of Susannah, anymore. For two years, Wrenda had acted as a mother to Susannah. Every day, Wrenda felt her heart warmed and expanded.

The store held a black dress that Wrenda would wear at Susannah's funeral. Not yet. I'm not going to buy that dress and start saying goodbye. *She thought.*

The sob started deep inside Wrenda, and it leaked out in sound and in tears.

She looked up and Marta sat near her, silently offering her some tissue for her eyes.

Wrenda looked at the brooch in her hand.

"You still have it," Marta said.

"It's been …

"Ten years."

"You're a good friend," Wrenda said. Their friendship had begun with those tissues. Marta had no idea that around 233 years earlier, that Wrenda had poisoned her with The Madness. Caused her to destroy her husband, Ethan.

In her peripheral vision, Wrenda saw rain pelting her cabin window. The Helios floated through a storm.

Rain. Wrenda saw rain pelt the skylight over the bench she sat on. Somehow, the whole shopping mall looked gray.

That day, as Marta handed a tissue to her, Wrenda saw Marta in a new light. Marta was no longer the 17-year-old-girl who had caused her son, Lord Wu, to kill himself.

Perhaps, grief was emptying out Wrenda's heart. Clearing her eyes.

After giving her the tissue, Marta had accompanied her new acquaintance, Wrenda, into the store. Wrenda got the dress, and a black wrap.

Marta purchased the brooch to pin the wrap together. A day later, together, they stood side by side at Susannah's funeral. Wrenda wore the black dress with the brooch holding her wrap together. Marta held the umbrella over both their heads. Rain on the funeral. Rain in Wrenda's heart.

Tears flowed down Wrenda's face. Still weak from her wounds and the less potent blood bank blood, Marta remained at rest in the pillows. She reached out and held Wrenda's hand.

Chapter 18

Mal hated waiting. Man of action. That's what he liked and aspired to be. He stretched his arms and loosened his shoulders. He caught Sable giving him what looked like an appreciative glance.

In the time since the death of his dear wife, Alicia, Mal had worked out some of his despair and aggression by pumping iron. His body took to the weightlifting as if born to it. His body responded by getting huge and wide. Still, at nearly seven feet tall, with bulging muscles, Mal stood as the epitome of masculinity. At least, that what he saw in the eyes of certain women.

He could see Sable almost shrug off her interest in him.

"Tonight. That's when my contact on the Helios will deliver the three artifacts of the Obscurum," Sable said.

Mal smiled. "You've done well."

What was that? Sable, in return, gave Mal a smile.

* * * * * *

Later that night, Marta fell in and out of consciousness. She had been advised to stay in the Healing Center—for observation. She slept but she bounced back into semi-consciousness at times.

She saw Dr. Lethem holding some objects and walking past her door. A cylindrical object stood out among the others. Wait! What was Dr. Lethem doing with Flute of Nightmares? And what were the other objects? Was that the Silent Scepter? Was that the Sword of the Dark Bloom in a sling hanging from Dr. Lethem's left shoulder?

I should get up. Got to get up, Marta told herself. But she couldn't move. Maybe I'm dreaming. Maybe I'm just in that paralysis-state that people get into as they sleep.

Marta fell into a deeper sleep.

Dr. Lethem checked Marta's vital signs and the monitors that were attached to her.

"Dr. Lethem, what were you doing with the Sword of the Dark Bloom?" Marta asked.

"You were dreaming," Dr. Lethem said. *Marta has seen me. She's not a member of my Helios family. I'll have to silence her,* Dr. Lethem thought.

Dr. Lethem opened a locker in the adjoining room. She pulled out an oakwood spear somewhat longer than three feet. An ideal weapon against a number of forms of vampire.

From the doorway, Dr. Lethem saw that Marta had drifted back to sleep.

This will be easier than I thought.

Dr. Lethem crept closer and closer to Marta's bedside.

She pulled back the spear and thrust the spear to skewer Marta in the chest.

But at that moment, a kick knocked Dr. Lethem to the side.

The oakwood spear pieced Marta's shoulder.

She screamed in agony.

Wrenda did a palm strike to Dr. Lethem's face, but the physician held onto the spear.

Marta was left bleeding from her wound.

Dr. Lethem simultaneously changed into Lycan form—

more strength and speed—as she jabbed multiple times at Wrenda. Wolf-Dr. Lethem expertly wielded the spear.

Wrenda took a blow to her gut. Growling, wolf-Dr. Lethem shoved the spear through Wrenda—the bloody tip emerging from her back.

Tremendously powerful, wolf-Dr. Lethem shoved Wrenda into a wall, pinning her there. Wrenda's mouth hung open, her elongated incisor teeth, betraying her vampire nature.

Marta struggled to her feet. Hopelessly defeated by her previous wounds and the new wound, left by the oakwood, she could not stand. She saw that her cell phone had been knocked some feet away. She needed to call for help.

Wrenda lifted her right hand, did a martial arts strike and broke the spear in half.

Now free to move, Wrenda gave every ounce of her spirit and energy to use a series of martial art strikes, pummeling wolf-Dr. Lethem.

Wrenda stared into wolf-Dr. Lethem's eyes and said, "You have betrayed your profession and the crew of this ship. You are the lowest."

Snap! Wrenda broke Dr. Lethem's neck. With her eyes open and a face of self-disgust, wolf-Dr. Lethem died.

Wrenda collapsed.

Marta crawled on the floor to Wrenda, leaving a trail of her own blood.

Marta grabbed the cellphone from the floor, dialed and said, "Healing Center. An attack—get Mrs. Chi—crew member down. Dying," Marta gasped.

Marta dropped the cellphone so she could cradle Wrenda.

"I—I'm sorry," Wrenda said.

Marta, for the first time, saw the elongated incisor teeth. *Wrenda is a vampire? How did I not know this?* Marta immediately pulled the oakwood out of Wrenda's gut.

"I'm sorry," Wrenda said again.

"What? No—no, hang on," Marta said. "We'll have Mrs. Chi put you into some spell to—"

Wrenda smiled, still finding it hard to talk. "I'm glad I got to know you. It has been an honor to be your friend."

Marta hugged Wrenda to her.

Into Marta's ear, Wrenda whispered, "Out, out brief candle."

"No! You have time. We have time," Marta said.

"When you know … please forgive me." Wrenda breathed out one last breath.

A sob rose from Marta's heart. Her dear friend was gone. *She was a vampire. She never told me. Forgive her for what?* Marta felt confused.

Mrs. Chi arrived.

Marta whispered, "Oakwood. Wrenda is a vampire. I—"

Mrs. Chi did a spell, flushing out the wound in Marta's shoulder. The spell seized a couple of oakwood splinters.

"You are free of the splinters. You will heal," Mrs. Chi told Marta.

Assured that Marta would live, Mrs. Chi looked to Wrenda, still in Marta's arms.

"I will wait outside. Call me when you are ready," Mrs. Chi said.

Left alone with Wrenda's body, Marta sensed some type of vibration. Then Wrenda's body dissolved to dust … and then nothing.

Marta shook, trying to absorb the shock at seeing her friend's body vanish.

Marta thought, *How will I ever be ready to carry on without Wrenda?*

Chapter 19

"I'm sorry that I got intense about—" Jenalee said.

"It happens," Noah said, as he sipped his coffee.

Jenalee nodded, then took a drink of her orange juice. The Grand Hall stood mostly vacant.

"… I don't know when I can handle this. I just—I screw up so bad. I trusted Trin. And she had been sure. But she had been fooled. And … I should have realized Gram-Gram was going to let me get away, and she planned to slow down Mal."

"How can you know everything—and what she *might* do?" Noah asked.

"I should have known that Gram-Gram would sacrifice herself," Jenalee said.

Noah opened his mouth to say something. Then he just listened. Jenalee saw that.

"Noah, you know, you're pretty smart.

"How's that?"

"You know when to shut up and just listen," Jenalee said. "That's what I really need. Except probably I need somebody to shake me up, too—sometimes."

"Oh, yeah. Then how am I supposed to know what to say or not to say at a given moment?" Noah said.

"Being my boyfriend is kind of tough on you, isn't it?" Then her eyes went wide. "I mean well, uh, we're like friends, right?"

Noah nodded vigorously.

She looked at Noah and then kissed him. It was a good kiss. They leaned into each other. They held that way for a good long time.

Some moments later they walked down a corridor, holding hands. Daniel exited the elevator and saw them. He turned right around and got back on the elevator.

Jenalee called, "Daniel." But she didn't stop holding Noah's hand.

Noah took this as a truly good sign.

Sahkeisha found Daniel at the SkyLevel. He shook, furious. "How could she do something like that? Take up with his Noah guy? When I was sick," Daniel said. "I got sick on a mission with her. I was risking my life for *her* purpose. I was following her lead. Well, that's enough of this. I should go back to my real life. I'm supposed to be an engineer. This whole thing was a stupid idea. I put my life on hold for what? For a stupid..."

"You seem to have a real appreciation for the word stupid," Sahkeisha said.

"Don't do me any favors," Daniel said. "You know nothing you're going to say can make any of this better."

"You got that right. When it hurts, it hurts," Sahkeisha said. "And no stupid words fix it. It's like having your chest cut open and someone hands you a Band-Aid."

"Okay. You sound like you've had your heart ripped out of you, too."

"More than once. I do have something to add here. You care about Jenalee. Caring about somebody, maybe even loving them is *not* stupid."

"Yeah, yeah," Daniel said.

"I don't know if this will do you any good. But I want you

to know that I can see that you're a good person. And I don't know, maybe, your time with us is done," Sahkeisha said. "But you've been an important part of our team here. And if this is the end of a chapter of life. It's been a good chapter. Anyway, what do you want now? To be by yourself? Or for me to get you an ice cream sundae at the Grand Hall."

"I think it's time for the big guns—ice cream sundae, Twinkie, apple pie. With a bourbon chaser," Daniel said.

"All right. Do you want to take a walk before or after you gorge yourself?" Sahkeisha said.

"Better do it now," Daniel said. "—I don't know if I'll be able to move later."

Chapter 20

I heard about Marta's loss of her friend, Wrenda. I hadn't liked the vampire. But now, she seemed somehow human to me.

As I passed a door to the Grand Hall, I saw Marta sitting near the window. Just looking out the window at the clouds. Almost as if she was looking, waiting and watching for her friend, Wrenda, to miraculously return.

Wrenda had been a vampire. How could that have been?

And how could she have survived?

While Marta went back to rest in the Healing Center, I went to Mrs. Chi.

"I think I've figured out how Wrenda could survive among the Helios crew. A vampire—a wolf among the sheep—but not attacking any."

"And?" Mrs. Chi said. She sat back in her customary chair in her Ready Room aboard the Helios.

"She had Dr. Lethem procure extra blood bank blood," I said.

"Well said," Mrs. Chi said. "And it is possible that Wrenda had some leverage on Dr. Lethem."

"And that would have been?"

"Perhaps, Wrenda threatened to reveal Dr. Lethem's secret—that she was a Lycan."

"You have no Lycans on the crew?" I asked.

"None that I know of," Mrs. Chi said.

"Do you—do you have a prejudice against Lycans?" I asked.

'Not in particular. However, Lycans, like vampires, have certain requirements."

Then Mrs. Chi nodded to herself.

"What?" I asked.

"Certain details are clearer now. Dr. Lethem tended to eat alone in her office. I thought it just a quirk. Now we know ... she hid her dietary ways."

"She would have had live prey brought aboard the Helios?"

"She was with me for five years. She always ordered medical supplies. Perhaps, she had certain vendors who also provided for her special requirements."

Mrs. Chi shuddered. That was a first. I hadn't seen her do that before.

"Are you okay?"

"I ... I miss her. And, the circumstances of her death are ... painful," Mrs. Chi said.

"She attacked one of our allies," I said.

"And she didn't trust me to value her enough to ... to work something out related to her nature."

"Maybe, she just couldn't let you know that—"

Mrs. Chi blinked her eyes, startled about her own thoughts. "No!"

I remained silent.

"This is ... I really have no word for it," Mrs. Chi began. "My husband was killed. Torn apart by a Lycan. And ... and ... Dr. Lethem had worked at that hospital."

"She killed your husband?" I asked.

"Possible. I'll have one of my agents see if he or she can confirm what shift Dr. Lethem worked that day. It was five years ago, though."

"Why attack Marta?" I asked.

"She may have known something—"

Mrs. Chi's phone rang.

"I—I feel I must take this," Mrs. Chi said and answered the phone.

A few moments later, she ended the call.

"Marta—she's still in the Healing Center. And she just told me that she saw—" Mrs. Chi dialed a number. "Ensign Esperanza go to the Stronghold and double-check that the three artifacts of the Obscurum are still secure."

Just six minutes later, Mrs. Chi's phone rang.

"I see. Thank you, Ensign. For the moment, keep this information confidential. I'll tell Captain Yang myself. That is all." Mrs. Chi ended the call.

"The artifacts are gone," Mrs. Chi told me. "Dr. Lethem evidently delivered them from the Helios to someone."

I felt a deep burning in my gut.

I just knew that Mal Pala had something to do with Dr. Lethem betraying us.

"I just can't understand how a person with such a strong character as Dr. Lethem could have succumbed to being blackmailed, and then she gave up the three artifacts of the Obscurum," I said.

"You have heard me say there is no dishonor in being outmatched. You might also say that every person has a breaking point. We hope that we have mighty companions who can shore up where we are weak. And we can shore up where they are weak. But who knows what destiny has in store for us?" Mrs. Chi took a breath. "Dr. Lethem could not face the agony of losing her Helios family. She thought what she did was unforgivable."

"She could not face the agony ..." I echoed.

Mal would have three parts of the Obscurum. He'd come

after Jack next for the Cross of Sighs. And we were down. Marta down, Jack down.

This was bad.

Shit!

Chapter 21

Still in his titanium cage, Jack looked forward to seeing Marta. Still recovering, she entered the room where Jack was isolated.

"How are you feeling?" Jack said as Marta took a seat near him—with the cage bars between them.

"Like somebody's playing racquetball with my head."

Marta looked in Jack's eyes. "I... I was wondering. Interested in going dancing again?

Jack smiled. "Sounds like..."

"A date?"

Jack nodded.

Marta reached for his hand through the bars of the cage.

* * * * * *

With his bare hand, Mal took hold of the Flute of Nightmares, and the image of Alicia, his deceased wife, appeared before him. More vivid than before. Alicia had maggots piercing her beautiful face, but Mal desperately wanted to see her in any way possible.

"What are you staring at, Mal?" Sable asked.

"None of your business!" Mal's tone was savage.

Sable's right hand automatically began rising—just a moment from tossing a bolt of magical energy at Mal's head. And—

Sable let her right hand drop.

From the look on Mal's face just a moment ago, whatever he was seeing tore his heart apart. So Sable gave Mal a pass, for this moment.

Mal put the Flute of Nightmares down on his desk.

Sable instinctively went to pick it up.

"Don't touch it!" Mal said.

"That's it. You become respectful or—"

Mal got smart. He sat down in his chair and lowered his voice. "I meant that as a warning to protect you from harm."

Sable took a chair herself.

"The Flute of Nightmares is aptly named. If you touch it, I guarantee it will harm you," Mal said.

"Then why do you touch the thing?" Sable asked.

"I—I must see … someone who died."

"Your wife?"

"You know?"

"You think I would not look into someone I am working with?"

"Makes sense. You are extremely intelligent, Sable."

"… thank you," Sable said.

"My wife. I get to see her. But her face. Marred by squirming maggots. Piercing her flesh."

"There is a price for everything," Sable whispered.

"What?"

"There is a price for everything."

Mal looked at the Flute of Nightmares. "I am willing to pay it. For us to accomplish what's necessary with the Obscurum—we will have Jack and Jenalee pay, too."

Sable poured two glasses of high-end brandy.

She handed Mal a glass.

They clinked glasses.

Soon, Jack and Jenalee would be in the fight for their lives.

Chapter 22

Jack AngelSword woke up spitting out dirt. Facedown on the dirt, he rolled on his back to see trees of some forest looming over him. *Where the hell am I?*

The last thing he remembered was being on board the Helios, talking to … Marta. That's right.

He shook his head trying to become alert. The forest appeared filled with lush green foliage. Even birds singing in the trees. He probably would have felt quite peaceful here, but at the moment he could feel the Beast inside raging about how he was stuck in nowhere. The Beast knew Jack could have all the power possible in the world if he just used the pages of sacred text to find the Judas Gauntlet.

"Jack AngelSword," a voice called out from above him.

He glanced up and saw a truly fit, thin older woman perched on a tree branch. About fifteen feet above him.

"I invite you to take a deep breath. Perhaps, rise to a seated position. Calm yourself."

"Where am I?" Jack demanded.

"You're safe. This is my forest."

"Doesn't the forest belong to everyone?"

"Perhaps on an existential scale *yes*. However, this is a private preserve that belongs to my Academy," she said.

"You still haven't answered my question."

"Let's just say you're somewhere in Asia."

"How did I get here?"

"Your friends brought you here."

"I don't understand. Why would they just leave me here?"

"Before I answer your questions, I think it's best that I introduce myself. My name is Shuren Kato."

An impatient frown took over Jack's face.

"Some refer to me as Master Kato. If this turns out as I think it might, you would ultimately refer to me as sensei."

"Which means teacher," Jack said.

"Ahhh. Yes. With your studies of comparative religion, you do have more exposure to various cultures than some of the students who come to me."

"Your students? Would one of them be Trin?"

"Yes."

"Are we going to keep this conversation up—with you in the tree."

"For now."

Jack rose to a seated posture. "I'm not sure about this. I don't see how Jenalee would have trusted Trin after the whole disaster when she thought Master Haito was … Well, it turned out that Master Haito was really both a demon and the leader of the House of Dagger."

"Oh. You do have some memory."

"Just certain images." Suddenly, Jack felt his arms and hands tightening. Now with two fists, Jack's face and tone became harsh. **"I am done talking with you, old woman. I want to leave."**

"So the Cross of Sighs now takes over your voice."

"There are things I want to do."

"I'm sure you that is true," Shuren Kato began. "And I'm speaking to that which is in the Cross of Sighs. I am sure you have some plans. What might they be?"

"I will not tell you, old woman. You said that Jack's

friends brought him here. Where are they?"

Shuren Kato smiled. "I wanted to see what exactly I will be working with."

"I'll show you what you're working with." The Beast within Jack growled—as it tore off the Aren Shroud from Jack's left forearm.

In a flash, the tattoo on Jack's left forearm manifested as the AngelSword in Jack's right hand. He swung the sword and tore out a major chunk of the tree in which Shuren Kato perched.

The tree tipped, and Shuren Kato gracefully leapt to another tree.

"This won't do," she said. "I won't have you injuring my forest."

She tossed down three bulbs. Jack dissolved two bulbs with a flash of his AngelSword. But the third bulb got through and expelled a form of fast-acting gas.

Jack was unconscious before his face hit the dirt.

Again, Jack spit out dirt.

"This is getting old," Jack sputtered.

"Jack, you'll have a better time if you surrender to the process. To the training," Trin said.

Jack startled, realizing that he was trapped in some kind of rig that held his left arm behind him. He could not even twist and remove the Aren Shroud with his teeth.

"You've lost a week, Jack," Jenalee said.

"Wait. How did Trin convince you to trust her again after the disaster with her Master Haito. I mean, VoSkhar, the leader of the House of Dagger?"

"That's a long story," Jenalee began. "We don't have time for it right now. We're going to need to leave you here with Shuren Kato. So that you can get well and become free of the

Cross of Sighs."

"Mal has the Flute of Nightmares," Trin began. "—the Silent Scepter and the Sword of the Dark Bloom. Mrs. Chi needs all hands on deck to track him down and prevent him from getting the Judas Gauntlet."

Jack's eyes went wide, showing his concern.

"So, you get better," Jenalee said, a catch in her throat. She put her hand on his shoulder.

Trin kissed Jack's cheek and said, "You can beat this thing with Master Kato's help. You'll get free of the Cross of Sighs. Then you'll be back in action—I know you will. You take care, Jack." Tears glistened in Trin's eyes.

Jack nodded.

Trin and Jenalee got in a vehicle—like a car, but much more. The vehicle had been named a Cheetah, fast with extra options that made it fast over rough terrain, too.

"What is this thing with your mother having vehicles named after animals and then making sure that they look like the animal?" Jenalee asked.

"Ask her," Trin said.

"Will Jack really be all right?" Jenalee asked.

"I … I'm not sure. He'll have to confront his personal demons. Not everyone can take it. He could lose his connection to reality."

"You mean?"

"Yes. He could lose his mind."

Chapter 23

The Helios hovered above a street on the outskirts of a rural town in Japan. Captain Yang ordered that the Cheetah-vehicle retrieval elevator car be lowered.

Soon, Jenalee and Trin exited the elevator to find Noah waiting. Trin ducked away, and Noah stepped briskly to Jenalee.

They hugged. Jenalee felt comfortable in Noah's embrace.

Then she looked up and saw Daniel approaching.

"Uh—Daniel. You doing good?" Jenalee said.

Daniel approached. And Jenalee and Daniel had an awkward hug.

Jenalee invited Sahkeisha to take a stroll on the SkyLevel. They glanced out the open areas made by the movable panels. The passing clouds and breeze made for an invigorating walk.

"I don't know what to do," Jenalee said to Sahkeisha.

"Of course you don't. Daniel and Noah both have good qualities," Sahkeisha said.

"What would you do?" Jenalee said.

"Sorry, I've never had this situation. I've never had such abundance," Sahkeisha said. "It's always been one at a time—not that my pickings were slim."

"Do you believe in a soulmate?" Jenalee asked.

"I want to," Sahkeisha said.

"Of course, you do—you have Elyse," Jenalee said. "How's it going with you and Elyse?"

"Don't change the subject."

"It's all the same subject," Jenalee said.

"All right. I'll answer the question briefly, but then it's back to you," Sahkeisha said. "I trust this—this relationship with Elyse. Because we've had our fights, but we keep coming back to each other closer. Stronger. This is the third thing that I've trusted in my life."

"What three things?" Jenalee asked.

"You and me—our friendship. My music ability. And now my relationship with Elyse," Sahkeisha said.

Jenalee sat down on a bench at the bow of the Helios.

"It's good to hear you say that," Jenalee said. "I wonder when I'll know something for certain. I really wish I could catch a break."

Daniel strode up to Jenalee and Sahkeisha.

"Jenalee, I've got to talk to you about something," he said.

"Time for me to check-in on Elyse," Sahkeisha said, rising to her feet.

Jenalee looked intently at Daniel. Then, she glanced at Sahkeisha. "Right. Let me know how Elyse is doing, okay?"

Sahkeisha nodded.

As soon as Sahkeisha moved out of earshot, Daniel blurted, "I've got to go."

"What? Now? We need you," Jenalee said.

"'We need you.'"

"I need you to help–"

"That's it then."

"What?"

"You need me to help," Daniel began. "To be on your team. But what you're *not* saying is ... You need Noah."

"Sure. He's on the team.

"Let's cut the bullshit. I've seen you two. You fit. Like peaches and cream. Like chocolate and peanut butter—"

"You're not going to start a commercial here—"

"Damn it, Jenalee!"

"I'm—I'm sorry. I don't know what to say—I don't know what to do."

"There is nothing to do. Nothing for you to do," he said.

Jenalee noted the determined look on Daniel's face.

"I'm going back. I'm going back to college. Complete my education.

"I—"

"Look, you're like somebody who discovers they're a world-class singer," Daniel began. "Now is the time for them to sing. Sure, they could take some online classes. But the world needs them to sing. They need to do everything to sing."

Jenalee had tears well up. "You're my friend."

"That … that's true. But … this life. This sort of 'save the world-agent' life. That's not me. And you know it."

"But the team—"

"You ever heard of lean and mean. You'll get Jack back. You're going to be all right. Marta will get back on her feet. Think of it as a changing of the guard. I'm retiring, and Marta's taking my place."

"No one can take your place. In my heart."

"That's nice, Jenalee. That's nice." Daniel spun on his heel and darted away to his room. To pack up and go.

* * * * * *

In Prague, in a man-made cave below the Jesuit Church of St. Ignatius, Sable rather enjoyed tossing around the guardians of certain sacred texts. These Jesuits were dedicated to keeping the Judas Gauntlet from falling into evil hands, and they tried to stop Sable from getting the sacred text that gave clues about the Judas Gauntlet.

Now, they collapsed near Sable, whose glowing hands and twisted smile lit up the underground chamber.

Sable had made the path clear for Mal who marched in with five of his own soldiers.

Mal strode up to a display and lifted a clear lid that covered the pages of the sacred text. He placed the pages into translucent vellum to preserve them. Mal glanced at the nine dead Jesuits—their blood splattered on the walls.

"It's stupid to leave a trail that Jenalee and Jack can follow," Sable said.

"So you killed them," Mal said. "Excellent."

Chapter 24

"You let him go?" Sahkeisha asked. "I mean, doesn't Daniel mean a lot to you?"

"Of course, he does," Jenalee said.

"It leaves a hole in our team, you know."

"He's not a prisoner. He wants a regular life. He's gone back to college." Jenalee took a breath. "He saw me with Noah. We were just hugging. 'Hey, welcome back.'"

"That's why."

"Why what?"

"Why Daniel left. He knows."

"Knows what? Will you just spit it out?" Jenalee said.

"You and Noah are the match."

"I've been asking you about this. You couldn't've told me this earlier?"

"Girl, you got to find things out like this for yourself."

"Lot of help." Jenalee frowned.

They were quiet for a moment. Then Jenalee winced.

"What?" Sahkeisha asked.

"A thought just occurred to me."

"Yes?"

"It's—it's going to be all right," Jenalee said to herself as much as to Sahkeisha.

"What is going to be all right?"

"Daniel is going back to college, but he'll be fine. Because I left Sable Cane in the InBetween."

"Sure. She's stuck in there."

* * * * * *

Hellene made sure the door was closed and then alighted on a table near Sable.

In spite of herself, Hellene did enjoy the opulence of Mal's estate.

In her private room, Sable relaxed. Hellene served as her trusted ally, so she felt comfortable.

Being around Mal took some energy out of her. She had to be on her toes. The guy walked around like a rolling pile of hurt. But didn't he have the right? He wanted to see his dead wife so badly that he would somehow tolerate seeing her face, riddled with flesh-piercing maggots.

"You're thinking about him," Hellene said.

"Who?"

"Mal."

"Really. I could be thinking of something else."

"Daniel, perhaps?"

"Not at the moment. Not all the time."

"I thought as much. You're not having us monitor him."

"Why should I?" Sable asked. "Daniel is now under the protection of Mrs. Chi. And his home is now the Helios. I have no interest in tangling with Mrs. Chi and her minions until we have suitable power."

" — provided by the Obscurum," Hellene said.

"Yes."

"It doesn't answer the question."

"What question?"

"Is your goal to change reality still — to capture the heart of Daniel?"

Sable paused. "I am ... I am considering a number of

things."

Hellene bowed to Sable. "Mistress, I thank you for this conversation."

"You've earned my trust. There is no one in this universe who sought to save me from the InBetween, other than you."

"I remain grateful, Mistress, that you intervened on my part and saved me from the torture of Khodan."

"And what is it do *you* want, Hellene?"

"I have entertained the idea that meeting out torture upon Khodan would be... delightful," Hellene said with a smile.

"So be it. Depending on how situations turn to our advantage ... Perhaps, we might get you that opportunity to meet out justice upon Khodan. As my gift to you," Sable said.

"Thank you, Mistress."

* * * * * *

"Zara," VoSkhar said, in his secret chamber of his second favorite estate. He didn't even put on his VoSkhar image. He wanted Zara to see his demon-Khodan form. His vicious eyes. Sharp teeth. The maniacal grin that came easily to his face. The pointed ears. He did not yell. Yelling would make him sound like a weak human.

His quiet intensity made him terrifying.

"What form of demon am I?" Khodan-VoSkhar said. He held his open claw below her face.

"T-Trenklin." Zara coughed and writhed in the restraints. He closed his fingers slowly.

"You have heard and sometimes seen what I can do to someone who crosses me."

Zara nodded. If she opened her mouth, she might just whimper. Khodan-VoSkhar liked obedience but not weakness.

"What to do? You have defied an order from me."

"It was not—" Zara choked on her comment. Khodan-VoSkhar's simple move with his index finger caused her continued pain. A Trenklin demon wielded levels of magic beyond the imagination of soldier-demons—the lowly Ongma demons.

"You were going to say that it was not premeditated. That is what saves you. And, your years of loyal service. Your usual competence and loyalty are rare," Khodan-VoSkhar said.

Khodan-VoSkhar waved his hand. The restraints on Zara's arms and legs got red hot and then fell off. Zara fell to her knees.

"See that you do *not* disappoint me again."

With relief, Zara looked up. "Thank you, sir."

Chapter 25

"Run!"

Jack AngelSword looked ahead to see Shuren Kato running gracefully in front of him.

"I am running."

"Not fast enough." She pulled away—through the forest.

Jack poured on his effort. He remained astonished at Master Kato's fitness. She looked fifty. But she had the wise countenance of someone older.

"Is this necessary?" Jack asked.

"You'll see."

Jack's breathing became hoarse.

Now Jack felt irritated.

Or was it the Beast inside him that started to fume?

Jack glanced at his right forearm and saw the Cross of Sighs glowing.

He felt desperate to be free of the clutches of the Cross of Sighs.

Desperation will not help you.

Where did that voice emanate from? Jack thought. He glanced at his right forearm—the Cross of Sighs had something in it. Something evil.

Jack stopped and leaned against a tree. Panting heavily. So hard to breathe.

"I see it in your face. You realize something," Shuren Kato said.

Jack watched his hand dart out in an attempt to grab her neck. Shuren Kato easily ducked out of the way.

"No. It's not me," Jack said.

"I know. This is not my first encounter with someone afflicted with the Cross of Sighs," she said.

"Then you can get me free."

"I point to the path. It is you who must traverse it," she said.

"You will not defeat me again." The Beast of the Cross of Sighs used Jack's voice to communicate.

"It is truth that defeats you," Shuren Kato said.

"What truth? Who's truth?"

"You seek to deny Jack's essence. He is *not* rage," she said.

"No. You don't see what I see."

"Tell me, Jack. What is the source of your hate?" Shuren Kato asked.

"I do not hate," Jack said.

"That is what you tell yourself."

"Because it is true!" Jack said.

"Run!"

"I can't."

"You can and you will. If... If you want freedom."

Jack summoned his will. "I ... want ... my freedom."

Step after step. Now walking.

Step after step. Now jogging.

"I ... want ... to be ... me!"

"Good, Jack. Carry on."

Minutes passed. Jack ran.

Until—he came to a crashing stop and vomit his breakfast.

Shuren Kato stepped over to Jack. She had kept herself out of reach of his projectile vomit.

"Step away from there. Sit below this tree."

"I will not!"

"Jack, you assert yourself," Shuren said. "You have a choice here."

Jack attempted walking. He could not defeat the Beast. The Beast knew that it was getting closer to expulsion.

Jack crawled on his hands and knees.

He sat down in the spot indicated by Shuren Kato.

"Close your eyes."

Jack complied.

"Tell me how you feel."

"My skin—"

"Yes."

"Like it is covered in fuses attached to dynamite."

"True. They were inside. They are now on the surface."

"Make them go away. Help me. Please."

"You must stay strong, Jack. Trust the process."

"I trust you."

"I am here.

"How can I make the fuses go away?" Jack asked.

"It's called healing. You need certain experiences."

"What?"

"Experiences of love and peace," Shuren Kato said.

The Beast inside Jack expelled a rueful laugh.

Jack's eyes blinked open. But Jack asserted his will and closed his eyes again.

"Where are you hurting, Jack?"

Physically exhausted and open emotionally, Jack felt pummeled by a tornado of images and feelings from his past:

— *Mal punched Jack right in the face, tossing him back into a wall and his head struck the wall. Pain. All Jack's brother had for him was anger, jealousy and hate.*

— *Threatening the life of Jack's seven-year-old niece, Mal* clutched the dredaya, a small mystical object. Jack's heart hurt that he might not be able to save little Sydney's life.

– The magical force etched the AngelSword tattoo on Jack's arm. Searing pain. Jack accepted this burden, so he would be equipped to fight his brother and save his niece's life.

"Mal nearly killed a little girl—to bait me! I hate him!" Jack said.

Good, Jack. Revel in the hatred.

"There is more, Jack. Old pain. Deeper," Shuren Kato said.

More images—feeling the striking of blows—

– Jack sees his own 8-year-old face in a mirror just before his father grabs him by the hair and throws him into a wall.

– The ever-present stench of stale beer and bad breath. His father—face too close—spitting on little Jack

– Jack is on the floor, beaten, can't get up—sees his father punch his mother in the face

– Jack sees his mother in her rookie police officer uniform

– Sees his father grab a beer bottle and attack his mother. In her police uniform, she ducks and strikes his father in the throat. His father drops.

– Night. On the street. Spray painting "war" to make a stop sign read "Stop War." Sees his best friend Mark, 15 years old like Jack was. Mark holding a gun. Mark—blood spurting from his chest. Jack's mother running up. She is shocked."Told him to drop the gun."

– Mark dies.

– His mother continues carrying the gun—wearing the badge

– Again—blood—blood in Mark's mouth, spitting up. Mark dying.

– Father hits Jack, Father hits mother, Mother hits father, Mother shoots Mark—over and over and over

Jack fell backward. Writhing. Eyes scrunched tight. The pain. The agony. He wanted to run away. To escape. No escape. No release.

The Cross of Sighs glowed, enjoying all of Jack's anguish.

Chapter 26

Marta saw the elongated incisor teeth in Wrenda's mouth. She's a vampire. But how? I would have known. My closest friend. Ever. She hides this from me. Why?

Blood pouring out of the wound in Wrenda's gut.

Pouring.

Flooding.

Marta tearing her own sleeve off. Stop the bleeding. The cloth she's trying to use to staunch the blood. Drenched in Wrenda's blood. More blood pouring out around the cloth.

She's dying. My friend. Dying. Dying.

Darkness.

Wrenda's gone. Wrenda.

Nothing.

Just a hole in my heart.

Marta woke up from her nightmare, crying. Shaking.

She blinked her eyes open.

She saw Jenalee sitting at her bedside.

Marta felt the tracks of tears on her face.

"You saw? What did I say?" Marta asked.

"... Wrenda," Jenalee said.

"Then, you know."

"I ... I know that your close friend is —"

"—is dead. Is only with me in my dream. In her last terrible moments," Marta said. "I am left with a hole in my heart. And a terrible question."

"Which is? Oh, I'm sorry. I mean. We don't know each other well," Jenalee said.

"I'll tell you. You lead Jack. And I want to heal and help Jack. So, you could say, you lead me, too." Marta paused a moment. "The terrible question is: Why did Wrenda hide her vampire nature from me? We could have shared … Who was Wrenda, really?"

"I can't help you. I … maybe some clues would be in her room. I've requested that the room be maintained for you."

"Thank you," Marta said.

"I can't know what you're going through. Still, when I lost my Gram-Gram—my grandmother … she fell in … in battle. The pain was … The pain is a little quieter now. It is a brick that I carry with me."

Marta nodded.

"You look ill," Jenalee said.

"The blood bank blood. It impedes my healing."

Jenalee remained silent. Thinking.

"I have an idea," Jenalee said. "I don't think Mrs. Chi is going to like it."

Marta drank long and deep. The fresh blood coursing through her body. Healing her.

Not draining too much—not enough to kill the man. Almost. He would be dead in three days, anyway. Mrs. Chi had arranged this. The man was a convicted murderer and rapist. In the country he lived in—the death penalty was coming for him.

Mrs. Chi had arranged a detour for the prisoner. A detour to nourish Marta. Already, she could feel strength returning. Marta placed her hand on her side. The gashes placed by jaguar-Zara were healing. Soon, not even a scar would remain.

Marta had to hand it to Jenalee. She wanted her team intact. Especially with Daniel gone. Jenalee thought like a leader. Out of the box. Persuasive. Mrs. Chi apparently was stepping back a little. Almost like Mrs. Chi was, perhaps, grooming Jenalee. What was Mrs. Chi's full plan? Whatever it was, there would be ripple effects. Marta felt glad to be coming back to full, vampiric power. The cold war between the House of AngelSword, House of Dagger—and perhaps, even The Council, could erupt in a fiery war at any time.

Chapter 27

The battle raged on. A battle for Jack's soul. The Beast within reveled in Jack's pain, anguish, and the rage that rose from them.

"Make it stop," Jack said.

"This is necessary, Jack," Shuren Kato said.

"I can't take it."

"You must. The only path to freedom is through."

Jack thrashed around. His right hand went to claw at the Aren shroud, so that his Angel Sword could manifest. Shuren Kato moved swiftly, like a blur, as she hogtied Jack's hands behind his back. She placed mittens on his hands, so he had no chance to get at the Aren Shroud.

"Make it stop."

A tornado of images tormented Jack—

His father lifting him up by his hair and tossing him into the wall.

His father striking his mother.

His mother in her police uniform striking his father in the throat.

Blood spurting from Mark's chest.

Mark dying in Jack's arms.

His mother saying, "I said drop the gun."

His mother continuing to wear the badge and the gun, year-in and year-out.

Mark's birthday arriving—always the empty chair. Noah, that is, Mark's brother and Jack together raising a cup to acknowledge Mark's birthday.

A hole in Jack's life never to be filled due to Mark's absence.

All of these images reminding Jack—making him re-experience the aloneness.

Jack's own judgments against his father. Looking on his father's beatings as evil. You don't beat a child. And if you do it again and again, you are evil. Every judgment against his father as a mirrored judgment inside Jack. My father is evil. I come from evil—I am evil. All I can do is control myself and not descend into the disgusting hole of evil, my father revealed.

But the Cross of Sighs removed Jack's self-control. It removed who he thought he was.

"Evil! My father—cruel—evil" Jack said. "I'm like my father. Noah was dying. No hesitation. I cut people in half. Killed them. Killed for Noah. Killed for Jenalee. I chose. I fed the AngelSword, and it resurrected Noah and Jenalee. I just did it. The 20 people at Mal's estate. Just killed them. Not just killed. I was cruel. Vicious. Mindless. Not me." Jack shook in horror. "No, it is me. Evil."

Shuren Kato watched Jack's ravings.

He would come through this.

Or his mind would snap.

And he would be lost.

Chapter 28

Marta moved as a blur, past Jenalee and stood next to Noah in the Adversary Room.

Marta held both of Jenalee's fighting sticks in her hands.

"I hate it when she does that," Jenalee said.

Noah couldn't help himself. He laughed.

Jenalee stuck her tongue out at Noah.

"Hope you know how to use that thing,"

"Wouldn't you like to know."

Marta glanced at both Noah and Jenalee, then said, "Get a room."

"What?—uh—what?" Noah sputtered.

"So, Captain. You satisfied that I'm fit for duty?" Marta asked Jenalee.

"Yeah—yeah."

"Good. There's something I need to do. Maybe, you could—"

Moments later, Jenalee handed Marta a keycard as they stood outside the door to Wrenda's cabin.

"You ready for this?" Jenalee asked. She instinctively reached a kind hand to Marta's shoulder.

Marta did not recoil so Jenalee gently placed her hand on Marta's shoulder.

Marta had no words. She nodded.

As she pressed the door open, Marta listened. No squeak. *Not* like some hidden chamber in an old mansion.

The absence of the noise made the moment even more horrible for Marta.

Marta and Jenalee stepped in.

Jenalee made sure to shut the door.

"I've requested that this cabin be set aside as long as you prefer," Jenalee said.

Again, Marta had no words. Her eyes expressed her appreciation. She nodded.

Jenalee sat in a chair.

Marta looked around.

"When you find out, please forgive me," Wrenda said. Her last words.

Find out what? During the battle with wolf-Dr. Lethem, Wrenda had revealed her vampire nature. That could not be the thing to find out. There remained another secret.

Nothing to do but look through Wrenda's things.

The brooch that Marta had purchased for Wrenda had been found in Wrenda's pocket.

In fact, Marta wore that brooch now, on the lapel of her blouse.

Marta opened the nightstand drawer.

Maybe, Wrenda wrote in a journal.

No journal.

In fact, the room didn't have much in it. Wrenda held to a Spartan existence.

Strange to say Spartan. This reminded Marta that Wrenda had likely lived for centuries. At some time, Wrenda had learned some magical spells—something to disguise her vampire nature. More than that, she had attached to herself some form of spell that made her dissolve to dust upon her death. What did she have to hide?

And, had Wrenda learned anything else over the centuries?

And this secret—was it tied into Wrenda's past as a vampire. Was that why Wrenda didn't want Marta to know she lived as a vampire?

Marta opened a closet.

Blouses. Gifts Marta had given Wrenda. Ten blouses. A different blouse for every birthday Wrenda and Marta had celebrated together.

A small suitcase rested in the bottom corner of the closet.

Wrenda picked it up, placed it on the bed. Opened it. Some slacks. Piled neatly.

And below it … a framed photo of a painting.

Marta's keen eyesight. Saw the imprint of lips.

What? Had Wrenda been a consort of the man depicted in the painting—Lord Wu?

Unlikely. Marta as Lihau had kept tabs on the consorts of Lord Wu—saw them age and die.

Not a consort.

Could it be? Had Wrenda been …? She had centuries to learn shapeshifting techniques.

Wrenda always insisted on getting ten hours of sleep.

Being a shapeshifter—maybe living on blood bank blood. These affected Wrenda's energy.

Was Wrenda Lord Wu's mother?

Marta shivered.

"When you know, please forgive me," Wrenda said.

Then, Marta remembered Lady Wu's last words to her. "You will pay for the desecration of my son."

Then Lady Wu had vanished from history.

"Pay."

The muscles of Marta's neck tensed. Her gut went cold.

Wrenda—that is, Lady Wu—had dropped The Madness on Marta.

Had made Marta tear apart—to massacre—her husband,

Ethan.

"Forgive you?!" Marta yelled. She tore off the brooch, threw it, and it shattered a mirror.

Marta tore out of the room.

Jenalee thought of running after her.

Then, she realized. Marta needed something that Jenalee could not provide.

Chapter 29

"Breathe, Jack. In and out. Notice the pain. In your mind, sit *next* to the pain," Shuren Kato said.

Jack remained on his back. Trying to breathe. Attempting to slow down the rate of each inhale and exhale.

As he focused on his breath, the pain quieted down just a bit.

"Good, Jack. Focus. On your breath. You continue to sit next to the pain."

Jack, you *are* the pain. The pain *is* your rage. There is nothing else. The Beast said in Jack's mind.

"Jack, focus on my voice. Now open your eyes," Shuren Kato said.

Jack opened his eyes.

"Turn on your side. Rise up to a seated position," she said.

The effort caused Jack to sweat profusely. Sweat flowed down his face.

"Good. Now, look ahead of you. See the stream," she said. Then, Shuren Kato tossed a throwing star, a shurenken at an overhead branch. Four leaves fell and landed on the stream. The leaves flowed past Jack.

"See the leaves. Each of your thoughts is a leaf. You could pick up one leaf, hold it close to your eyes. Then, you'd obscure your vision. But there is more, Jack. You are more. You are not just one thought."

Jack nodded, just a bit.

You *are* one thought. When that thought is the truth. The only way to deal with pain is to overpower it. Hate the pain. Rage about it. The Beast said in Jack's mind.

"What am I trying to do here?" Jack grunted—through the difficulty to talk.

"Sit with the pain. You don't have to eliminate it. You accept it—" Shuren Kato began

"I do not accept it! I do not accept evil!" Jack said.

"Accept does not mean approve. I mentioned: Sit next to the pain. Sit next to it until it quiets down. Until fear quiets down."

"I'm not afraid."

"Is that true? Do you know that—deep down do you know that?" Shuren Kato said.

Jack said nothing.

Shuren Kato did nothing to disturb the silence.

Jack felt himself going deeper. A fleeting thought went by. Am I meditating?

In his mind's eye, Jack found himself on a sidewalk, riding a bicycle. Looking at his own hands, he didn't know how old he was.

About a half block away, his father clapped his hands. A moment of approval.

Gone. Replaced by his father yelling. It looked like anger distorting his father's face.

Jack couldn't hear him.

Was his father ... in pain?

In that moment, Shuren Kato plucked the Cross of Sighs from Jack's arm.

Deftly, Shuren Kato placed the Cross of Sighs into a bag and cinched the top.

The Cross of Sighs squirmed in the bag like a snake would before it quieted down.

Jack opened his eyes, glanced at his right arm. "I'm free."

Chapter 30

"I'm not cured, am I?" Jack said, looking Shuren Kato straight in the eye.

"What brings this to your thoughts?"

"Why is it always answering a question with a question?"

"Does this bother you?"

She smiled. Then, she laughed, and Jack joined her.

After a time, Jack looked downward.

"I am afraid," he whispered.

"Good. I would hope so," she said.

"Yeah. You're a lot of help."

Shuren Kato held up the bag with the Cross of Sighs trapped within. She pointed at the bag. Yes, she had helped.

Jack laughed. It was a big laugh, it felt good.

"Now, that laughter is exactly a good part of your process," Shuren Kato said.

"Really?"

"It is not about becoming perfectly at peace," she began. "I will teach you the loving-kindness meditation. You will have practice quieting down fear and hatred. You will *not* look to have an absence of all pain."

"Life is suffering—it is part of the Four Noble Truths of Buddhism," Jack said.

"Of course. I read your book on comparative religion. Good for what it is," Shuren Kato said.

"Everybody's a critic," Jack said, lightly.

"Jack, you have gone far deeper than you could at the time of your writing. The ordeal with the Cross of Sighs has done you a bit of good."

Jack looked skeptical.

"Fine. You are skeptical. That is not the same as being a cynic. To go to different levels, it is a matter of feeling, intuition, experience. Not just thinking. Not just the rational mind. There is more."

After some days in meditation and martial arts training, Jack felt stronger. Better than before.

Jack walked through the foyer of the main building of Shuren Kato's secluded Academy.

Trin stepped up to him. Jack broke into a big smile, happy to see her.

"So Jack, she took you to the forest." Trin said.

"How do you know?"

"You stink." Trin smiled.

"I run. I sweat."

"There are other ways to sweat. I mean—" Trin said. Then she smiled.

Trin looked at Jack's right forearm.

"It's good to see that you're free of the Cross of Sighs."

"It's even better to *feel* free."

Shuren Kato strode up to them. "Good progress, Jack. And—the loving-kindness meditation would be a practice to continue for your life. You had a moment of compassion. That is what made the difference. So I could remove the Cross of Sighs," she said, as she handed a strong box that held the deadly artifact.

"I'm sure that Mrs. Chi will want to secure this," Shuren Kato said. "You are a good student,"

Jack bowed to Shuren Kato. Trin also bowed. Shuren

returned the bow and stepped away.

"You hear that?" Jack said, grinning to Trin.

Some steps away, Shuren called over her shoulder. "Great kid. Don't get cocky."

Shuren kept walking to her next class of aikido students.

"She quotes Han Solo—of *Star Wars*?" Jack asked Trin.

Trin leaned over and kissed Jack on the cheek.

This unnerved Jack. "I—I'll be back." Jack stepped over to the restroom. He looked in the mirror. *What the hell am I doing? I'm somehow connected to Marta. I mean—well, I don't know if I could be a soulmate to a vampire or I mean, if she was hungry, would I be vampire chow?*

Trin and Jack left the sacred grounds of Shuren Kato's hidden martial arts academy.

Jack glanced at the strongbox in his hand. "She gave me the Cross of Sighs. Master Kato does not want to keep this artifact here in this hidden academy?"

"Perhaps, this is connected to why my mother and Master Kato stopped talking to each other."

"They were friends?" Jack asked.

"For decades. I'm guessing a difference in philosophy."

"Master Kato patched me up to go back into the field."

"She has no interest in entering the field herself." Trin led the way. They were silent for a time, striding through the hidden forest.

"Is the hidden academy shielded?"

"Yes. Protected from magical surveillance. That's why I knew you would be safe. Mal would not be able to track you down. Although, I'm sure that he wants the Cross of Sighs. That would add a fourth to the three artifacts he already has."

"I remember. He just needs all five artifacts—then he can

wield the full power of the Obscurum."

"My mother talked about the Obscurum. With all five artifacts together, the person could change reality across the 9 Realms."

Jack nodded. Then he glanced around. "You said that the hidden academy is shielded from magical surveillance. How about Google Maps?"

"Shielded from that, too."

"And the Helios has never been here?"

"That would break an agreement between my mother and Shuren Kato. What's with all the questions?"

"Thought I'd get the lay of the land."

Trin glanced at Jack.

He saw it. He felt that if he asked Trin the right question they would stop for a real pause that refreshes. And at that moment, he also remembered how Marta caressed his face—on the train when they first met. What did he feel in his heart? Which one? Who could he love? And what was love to a vampire? Like saying I love chicken?

"We're here," Trin said.

"What?"

"Where did you go?

"I'm right here."

"Your face. You had a strange look on your face."

"Really? Like what?"

"It was a frown. Like somebody pushing you into something you didn't like," Trin said.

"It was nothing. Before we get in that car—"

"My team member Curry left this car for us," Trin said.

"Curry—as in the spice?

"Tell you about that later. You'd like her, Jack."

"What? Is she hot?"

Trin frowned.

"Sorry. The line was just sitting there. I couldn't help it."

"I'd expect that from Noah. Not you, Jack."

Trin walked closer to the car.

"Shouldn't we check it. I mean—"

"Curry is my most trusted friend."

"I believe you! I just mean that someone could have arrived after Curry left. That someone could have tampered with—"

Jack watched as Trin held her hands together and sent out a beam of energy that went across the car and made it possible to see through the car. The spell functioned like an x-ray machine.

"It's clean."

They got in the car. Trin accelerated, and they raced off.

"Could you teach me that x-ray trick?"

"It's not a trick," Trin began. She glanced over at Jack.

Jack's eyes were rigid, like he was seeing something—not the road ahead.

"You've gone quiet. What's going on?" Trin said. Was Jack going back to some form of state when he'd been under during the Cross of Sighs's influence?

"I—I just see them. Those people I killed at Mal's estate," Jack said.

"That was the Cross of Sighs. Jack, that was *not* you," Trin said, urgency in her tone.

Jack was silent.

Trin waited. Perhaps, he would say more.

"I don't—" Jack began. "I don't know how I'm going to live with the memories. The people ... what I did."

Trin kept driving, looking ahead. Keeping them safe. Still, she glanced at Jack. She wanted to let him know that she would be here. He would be okay.

The car rocked, from an explosion. Trin wrestled with the

steering wheel, struggling to keep control of the car. A second air-to-ground missile barely missed Trin's car, and she glanced up to see an enemy helicopter overhead.

She gunned the engine.

The helicopter continued in its deadly pursuit.

"Hold on tight. We got to get to that tunnel ahead," Trin said.

Jack already clutched the armrest and his seat with both hands. Totally white-knuckling it.

Trin smiled. "Not bad for a first date."

"This is a date?" Still, Jack managed to toss back a smile.

A third missile caught the back of the car, and their world tilted.

Jack thought, *Relax into it. Like being in a judo throw.*

Then he didn't think anymore—as the centrifugal force and succession of impacts took away all conscious thought.

The car tumbled down the side of the mountain.

Chapter 31

Magical power in her glowing hands, Sable caused two baseball-sized spheres to levitate. Between the spheres, Sable looked across time and space to read critical sacred texts about using the Obscurum.

"That's it. The ultimate advantage," Sable whispered.

Then she heard footsteps. She closed the spell. She would keep the insight she had just gained as a secret from Mal. She had learned years ago that holding certain secrets consolidated her power. You never knew who might turn on you, so keeping your true intentions to yourself was the wisest course of action.

Did she trust Mal? Only as far as he would fall if she kicked him in the balls.

Mal stepped into the study.

Sable made sure to speak first. "I notice that you're not reaching for the Flute of Nightmares often," Sable said to Mal.

"I've got to keep a clear head," Mal said. "We're getting close. Only two more artifacts, and we'll have the full Obscurum."

"To change the reality across the 9 Realms," Sable said.

"I see you've read the sacred texts that we recovered," Mal said.

"Got a problem with that?" she asked.

Mal looked at Sable and said nothing.

This is a sly one. He doesn't run at the mouth. And I do not see him drinking or using drugs to excess. I'll watch him. She placed a little smile on her face.

"Something on your mind?" Mal asked.

"I—" Sable noted her cellphone. "I have an incoming text." She noted the message. "My contact—my mole on the Helios is dead."

"I see it on your face. It bothers you," Mal said.

"The loss of a good resource is ... disappointing," Sable said.

"True."

"So, Jack AngelSword has the Cross of Sighs. And have your agents located him?'

"No. And this is strange. In the last couple of days, I did some spells to see if I could magically locate Jack or the Cross of Sighs. Both have been off the grid."

"Strange indeed. Could they have stepped out of this realm—the earth, and could they have gone into one of the 9 Realms?"

"Not certain. I'll keep my agents on the lookout," Mal said.

Sable noted how Mal took a big breath. His chest expanded. Like a boxer ready and looking forward to the fight to come.

Sable always liked having the upper hand. She had seen something in the sacred text that would allow her to turn the tables on Mal. When Sable implemented the hidden insight, she could decimate anyone in her path. She'd start with destroying Jenalee Storm.

Chapter 32

Finally, Trin's car came to a rest, after tumbling down the side of the mountain.

Trin and Jack did not move. Blood oozed from a gash on Trin's forehead. Some blood flowed from Jack's nose.

The helicopter hovered overhead, and VoSkhar descended the 'copter's rope ladder toward the car. VoSkhar didn't go into the field much, so this experience felt rather exhilarating to him. At this moment, he kept his real identity as the demon Khodan hidden beneath his form of VoSkhar.

On the ground near the car, VoSkhar clearly saw both Trin and Jack unconscious.

He felt an itching in his right hand, alerting him to the presence of a mighty artifact. What might this be? Something certainly worth possessing.

VoSkhar waved his hand and a bag rose up, levitated out of the car, through the open window on Jack's side.

VoSkhar caught the bag in his hand.

Now to have some fun, VoSkhar thought. *Do I wave my hands and do a spell to have the roof of the car crush the life out of these two?*

Actually, to kill Trin would be a loss. She had been a good student. And she was also a beauty.

Oh, well.

VoSkhar raised his hands and —

Gunfire. The impact right next to VoSkhar's feet. As a

reflex he jumped back, searching for cover.

On the Helios bridge, Jenalee turned from the monitor to Mrs. Chi.

"Do we end VoSkhar now?" Jenalee asked.

"It may not be the most prudent action," Mrs. Chi said.

"Really?"

"We are not in a declared war with the House of Dagger at this point."

"How about we just 'talk' with him—?" Jenalee glanced back at the monitor. Both VoSkhar and his hovering helicopter were gone.

"A cloaking spell. Clever," Mrs. Chi said.

"I don't call it that."

Mrs. Chi looked at Jenalee.

"I call it a lost opportunity."

Trin returned to consciousness. Felt the soft bed below her. Blinked open her eyes and saw Mrs. Chi there, seated near her in her room in the Healing Center. The quiet hum of the Helios engines provided a comforting ambiance.

"Mom—"

"You haven't called me that for years," Mrs. Chi said, a catch in her voice.

"I know," Trin naturally raised up her hands, inviting her mother for a hug.

Mrs. Chi leaned down to hug her daughter.

"Oww," Trin said.

Mrs. Chi startled and backed away.

"I didn't say stop, Mom."

Mrs. Chi had tears in her eyes. She super-gently hugged her daughter.

"I have two new doctors. They did a scan. Nothing is

broken but—"

"I'm pretty banged up. Where's Jack? Is he okay?"

"You went so easy on, Jack."

"That's why you kept sending him."

Mrs. Chi raised her right eyebrow. Then smiled.

"You *are* sweet on him. He is not a bad match."

"Mom!"

From the doorway, Jack said, "Oh. You two seem to be having a moment."

"So, you survived," Trin said, with a sweet smile for Jack.

He stepped over.

Mrs. Chi took a step back to allow Jack to sit next to Trin.

"I'll be on the bridge," Mrs. Chi said, and she strode to the doorway and exited.

"I'm so glad you're okay," Jack said.

"I'm—I'm good."

Naturally, Jack and Trin held each other's hand.

"Hey, we survived our—" Trin began

"First date," Trin and Jack said together.

They laughed.

At the doorway, Noah saw Trin and Jack holding hands.

In his peripheral vision, Jack caught Noah's wide-open eyes and his expression.

Noah turned and did a big sneeze.

In the hall, Marta ducked back.

"Noah, anyone teach you to sneeze into your elbow?" Marta asked.

At that moment, Jack pulled his hand back from Trin's grasp.

Marta came around and through the doorway.

"You two look okay," Marta said.

Jack smiled and nodded.

Trin blinked and put on a small welcoming smile.

"You look strong," Trin said.

At the doorway, Jenalee stepped in. "We found a way to—to meet Marta's nutritional requirements."

"Really? You got volunteers?" Trin asked.

"I've had some visits with prisoners on death row," Marta said.

"Convicted, serial killers," Jenalee emphasized.

All were silent a moment.

"So, how about you two—" Jenalee nodded to Jack and Trin, "—get some more rest. And some hours from now, I'll call for a planning meeting. Mal is still out there."

"Worse than that, VoSkhar has the Cross of Sighs," Jack said.

"And Mal will find some way to get the Cross of Sighs," Jenalee said.

"Unless we beat him to it," Marta said.

Chapter 33

"What is it?" Zara asked VoSkhar at his second favorite estate.

"I called in favors and had some research done. It is the Cross of Sighs," VoSkhar said.

Zara approached the strongbox.

"Leave it closed," VoSkhar said. Zara pulled her hands back fast. VoSkhar stepped over to the strongbox and placed it into an additional box with a powerful lock. He placed the key in his wallet.

"What I've learned so far is that this artifact was seen, by our agents, as attached to Jack AngelSword's arm like a leech. It is a parasite. It exerts too much power. Certainly, I want neither you nor I to fall under its sway."

"Sir, if I may ask, what is your plan?" Zara asked.

"Zara, I see: you do not know if you have retained your place as my confidant. Such caution is wise. Still, you have been loyal and trustworthy—except for the one lapse. Look me in the eyes."

Zara complied.

"Will you attack Jack AngelSword without my approval?"

"With every amount of restraint I can deliver, I would follow your command," Zara began. "But I have discovered that the Beast inside me has found an easy outlet in my grief and my rage over how Jack AngelSword killed my brother,

Erik."

"That is a reasoned analysis. What is your solution?" VoSkhar asked.

"To be safe, I would take myself out of the area. If for some reason you found it necessary for Jack to remain alive, I must *not* be anywhere near him."

"My original plans called for subtlety," VoSkhar said. "But now, since Jack and his associates know my multiple identities, subtlety is *not* called for. I now command that you destroy Jack AngelSword when he is next available to you."

"Thank you, sir!"

VoSkhar smiled.

Chapter 34

"You know we're going to be called into the meeting," Sahkeisha said, as she noticed the gentle hum of the Helios' engines.

"What meeting?" Elyse said, flexing her arm a bit.

"Go easy on that. You don't want to rip your stitches" Sahkeisha said.

"Yeah-yeah."

"We should get something to eat."

"As long as it's not tuna salad," Elyse said, referring to Sahkeisha's father's comment that choking on tuna and having a heart attack is "a stupid way to die."

"Did your father ever have a heart attack?" Elyse asked.

"No. Thank God," Sahkeisha began. "But my Dad did have a conversation with my mother. Picture this. My Dad said to my Mom. 'I want you to consider something. I'm 55 years old and there are some things I can't do anymore.'

My mother said, 'You're telling me this?'

My dad said, 'My knees don't work, so I can't run. And apparently, I can't eat food while walking. I got to sit my ass down and eat. But I'm going to ask you something. Would you consider *not* running outside and making me feel like I'm hurting you by making you wait? Could you just take a chair?'

My Dad looked her in the eye. And he added, 'And then we can take our walk. Would you consider that?'

And for once, my mother didn't say anything as a retort. She just went over and hugged my father. That was a good moment."

Elyse opened her arms and Sahkeisha fell into her embrace.

"I'd say that we're having a good moment," Elyse said.

They kissed.

* * * * * *

A few hours later, in the Helios' Ready Room, Jenalee rose to her feet. She looked over all the people assembled. She felt that Mrs. Chi, Noah, Sahkeisha, Jack, Elyse—this was her family. Maybe Trin and Marta were … well, whatever they were … they were on her team.

She felt grateful to see that Jack looked strong. Somehow both Jack and Trin had come through okay—even after the car crash, caused by VoSkhar.

"Jack, Trin, it's good to see you two doing well," Jenalee said.

"Thanks," Trin said.

Jack remained silent.

"Jack?" Jenalee asked.

"I … I've been thinking about this for a while. This VoSkhar—he has serious powers. He's probably worse than Mal. And he has the Cross of Sighs. And I… I might be liability," Jack said.

"What are you talking about?" Jenalee asked. "You're a good member of this team."

"And you don't know what you're talking about when it comes to the Cross of Sighs," Jack said. "I've succumbed to it before. If VoSkhar uses it on me, I don't know… I don't know what atrocity I might commit. It could worse than those people I massacred at Mal's estate in Italy."

"Why are you so busted about taking out twenty people who worked for Mal?

"I—I killed noncombatants. What would they have become?" Jack asked. "You think none of them could have done something later in life. Something better. You never heard of somebody coming out of prison and doing something good with their life? You don't think anybody can redeem themselves?"

Elyse said nothing.

Jack continued, "I mean, what would have my friend, Mark, done—if he could've lived beyond fifteen years? I did what my mother did—but I did it twenty times!"

Jack stood up and stomped out of the room.

Elyse turned to Sahkeisha and asked, "What's he talking about?"

"His mother, a rookie cop, accidentally shot Jack's best friend, Mark. They were just fifteen," Sahkeisha said.

"And I was twelve," Noah said. "Mark was ... Mark *is* my brother. He's just not here."

Noah stepped out of the room, too.

"Well, that went—" Jenalee said.

Sahkeisha added, "Well?"

"No. It went to hell."

"Maybe not," Elyse said. "Getting the truth out is a good thing."

Jenalee adjourned the meeting. She sought out both Jack and Noah in turn. And she got them to agree to return in thirty minutes to restart the meeting.

Once Jenalee, Mrs. Chi and the whole team were reassembled, Sahkeisha observed something in Jenalee's face.

"I've seen that look before. What's on your mind there,

Jenalee?" Sahkeisha asked.

"I'm thinking about the recent revelations. I think we've all talked about them in some way. Not only are we up against Mal, but we also have to contend with VoSkhar who is a much more powerful foe than we knew."

"So, he's a demon, right?" Noah asked.

"He's a high-level demon," Trin confirmed.

"Which means?" Noah asked.

"His command of magic is … terrifying. I learned my sorcery skills from him. And you know, that he reserved his best powers for himself," Trin said.

"And he's a shapeshifter," Marta said.

Jenalee nodded.

"His resources are vast as both a multi-billionaire with hundreds of companies and as the leader of the House of Dagger," Mrs. Chi said.

"I'm grateful that Marta, Trin and Jack—that you're okay now," Jenalee said. "We almost lost you three, and we have lost people on our team. Marta, I know you lost Wrenda and—"

Jenalee saw ghosts of Marta's feelings momentarily pass across her face. Still, Marta made her face go neutral.

Jenalee could not help pausing to look at her bracelet. Her Gram-Gram always knew Jenalee stood destined to use this magical shield bracelet. Gram-Gram may have known that she wasn't going to continue at Jenalee's side. *I miss you, Gram-Gram.*

Jenalee set her shoulders. "Mrs. Chi, I realize that it's hard on you to have lost Dr. Lethem," Jenalee said, her kind eyes on Mrs. Chi.

"And you lost Daniel," Sahkeisha said.

"Maybe lost isn't the word," Jenalee began. "He went back to his old life, back to college. Sahkeisha, remember college?"

"Oh yeah. that old thing. Next to my earlier chapter of life, my piano." Sahkeisha glanced at her right arm, that just hung at her side.

"That's right. Mrs. Chi, I'd like you to talk with Sahkeisha about helping her set up her own composing computer system and keyboards in her room."

Mrs. Chi said, "Perhaps, considering the space... Sahkeisha and Elyse would like to have a larger, living quarters together?"

Sahkeisha and Elyse smiled at each other.

Jenalee nodded.

"I've learned Sahkeisha shared a story shared with Elyse. Now, I'll share it with you." Jenalee squared her shoulders. "At one point, Sahkeisha's father was rushing out the door, eating a couple of spoonfuls of tuna salad at the same time. He got chest pains. He thought choking on tuna salad was a *stupid way* to die."

Sahkeisha nodded.

Noah's eyebrows went up.

Jenalee turned to Elyse, "I think you two now have a *code word*, right?"

Elyse and Sahkeisha said together, "Tuna salad."

"—which means 'let's not fall into some stupid way to die,'" Sahkeisha finished.

"My point is: I want to hear from all of us," Jenalee began. "We can be more strategic. I don't think risking a full assault on Mal's estate or VoSkhar's estate is our best leverage."

"You're calling that 'tuna salad,'" Noah said.

Jenalee nodded.

"With all of you—a group of really insightful, skilled and intuitive people—I think with all of us accessing intuition and strategic ideas, we'll think out of the box. It's about leverage. Thinking smarter than Mal and VoSkhar. So, let's talk about how we can do that."

"No problem. We have six women in this room," Sahkeisha said, smiling.

The meeting continued for two hours with one break in the middle of it. Jenalee felt better about how they would approach dealing with VoSkhar who possessed the Cross of Sighs. They also talked about how to deal with Mal who only needed the Judas Gauntlet and Cross of Sighs to complete his Obscurum collection. At the moment, they couldn't be sure how much power Mal already had with his possession of the Flute of Nightmares, the Silent Scepter and the Sword of the Dark Bloom.

Chapter 35

I really would feel better to talk to Daniel right now, I thought.

No. The first rule of a breakup is no phone calls.

Besides, we just had our big meeting, and I think the strategy is sound.

So, what's going on?

I miss Daniel.

If only he could just stay my friend.

But then, he went through a lot.

I mean he's safe now. I imprisoned his bat-shit crazy sister Sable in the InBetween. So now he can have a regular life. Complete his engineering degree. Get married. Raise 2.5 children.

All right who came up with that screwed up statistic? I don't want to see .5 of anybody.

Do I miss talking to Daniel or do I miss…

I got up, left my room and…

I wasn't finding the person I looked for—but I found myself near Sahkeisha's and Elyse's new suite together.

I marveled at how Mrs. Chi had things done within about two hours.

She treated our team like prized athletes.

I arrived outside Sahkeisha's door. I heard muffled music.

I knocked.

Sahkeisha invited me into the suite. Spacious.

"Elyse is out for her run. Maybe, she's walking because of recovering—" Sahkeisha said.

"What were you playing?" I asked.

Sahkeisha sat down at her music-making computer station. She had easy access to three keyboards. She could use her right hand, while her left arm just hung at her side.

Sahkeisha pressed a button on the computer keyboard. As the music played back, she sang:

If I only had the courage
to have purple hair.
But my boyfriend treats me like sewage
I would not dare.

"That's intense," I said.

"It's for my possible musical: 'Get Me Purple Hair.'"

"Sounding good."

"The next lines are:

Bitch-slap that boyfriend
Plaster his face on walls.
Kick him in the balls.

Sahkeisha smiled sweetly and said, "It's about empowerment."

I returned her smile.

Fifteen minutes later, I found Noah at the SkyLevel. I still loved how the Helios had the windows open. I could feel the breeze.

"You okay?" he asked.

"What?"

"I'm just asking. Just seeing how you are."

"I'm all right."

"Okay. I was just thinking about the 'I want to quit' thing you said to Sahkeisha—"

I'm going to take this up with Sahkeisha, I thought.

"Is this still going on for you?" Noah asked.

"I didn't ask for any of this," I said, sitting down on a bench near a lush, green tree along the track.

"So, what do you want to do about it?"

"What?"

"Your feelings about wanting to get free of ... of being our leader."

"I don't get it. Why doesn't Jack become the leader, now that he's back? Why doesn't he want to be the leader? Hell, his name is AngelSword."

"Maybe people fit together like jigsaw puzzle pieces. All this time, I don't see him volunteering to be the leader."

"Good for him."

"Meaning what?"

"He's not going to send anybody to their deaths." I ran out of steam there. I just shut up.

Noah sat there. Letting me just sit in my feelings. He's pretty smart.

He waited. He looked patient on the outside.

"Let's walk," I said.

We walked down the path, looking out the windows of this glorious SkyLevel.

"It's a good plan," Noah said.

"Oh? I thought you were going to wait and wait—until I said something."

"I went with my intuition. What? You want me to go through the plan with you now? Try to pick it apart?"

I must have frowned.

"I'm just asking. Is there something I can help with? Something you want from me?"

I grabbed him by his collar, pulled him to me and kissed him.

Chapter 36

"So I tossed the rubber ball, and it bounced off the wall, hit Jack in the head, bounced back to the wall and hit him in the head again," Noah said.

Jenalee laughed. Noah joined her. Jenalee glanced around the Grand Hall. Lots of crew were talking and laughing. *It's a good crew.*

"Then, Jack started to—" Noah said, continuing his story.

A spoon sailed through the air at Noah. He caught it.

"Good. You caught it. The cup was next," Jack said, as he put his food tray down and took a seat next to Noah.

"What's new to report?" Jack asked Jenalee.

"Mrs. Chi has her agents continuing to track—when they can—any movements of Mal and VoSkhar."

"It's a good plan. Your idea to set them up to fight each other," Jack said to Jenalee.

"Can I join you?"

Jenalee looked up to see Trin standing with her tray.

Jenalee paused for a fraction of a second—then nodded.

"Thanks," Trin said as she took a chair next to Jack.

Jenalee noted that.

So, did Jack. He gave Trin a smile.

"There's something I think we all need to take into account when we face Mal," Trin said.

"Yes?" Jenalee asked.

"Jack, you know that an evil entity pushed me to fight

you on the tower in Venice, Italy."

"Yeah," Jack began. "That guy—that thing—caused you to stab me."

"Uncle Richard. He is in another form. And he is now in the Sword of the Dark Bloom."

"With a demon that is already in there?" Jenalee asked.

"Yes, that demon took my eye."

"And the Ethereal Plane put your eye back? Healed you?" Noah asked.

Trin, Jack and Jenalee looked at Noah.

"Hey, I'm studying just like the rest of you," Noah said.

"So, what do we do about the Sword of the Dark Bloom—this double-trouble, two evil entities in that sword?" Jenalee asked.

"You've got to imprison them. But what would hold these non-corporeal beings?" Trin said.

"I saw that the Sword of the Dark Bloom—the hilt was tied down to the scabbard," Jenalee said.

"I did that," Trin said.

"So that works? The buggers can't get out?" Noah asked.

"Buggers?" Jenalee asked.

"No guarantee on that," Trin said.

"So, we got to put the sword into some substance. Maybe do some spell," Jenalee said.

"More homework," Noah said. He looked to Jack.

"Two *things* inside the Sword of the Dark Bloom. It just gets better," Jack said.

"I've been thinking about this," Trin said. "Master Haito turned out to be that asshole demon. But I've been working on magical studies beyond what I learned from him."

"Good to hear," Jenalee said.

"My mother said, 'There is no dishonor in being outmatched.'

"But do your damn homework." Mrs. Chi stepped up to their table.

Trin's eyes went wide.

Jack and Jenalee started laughing. Noah joined in. Trin smiled, and Mrs. Chi chuckled.

"You want to shove the entities back into the Sword of the Dark Bloom," Mrs. Chi said.

"Exactly," Jenalee said.

"Trin, I can help you with that ... if—"

"Sounds good, Mom," Trin said.

Now it was time for Jack, Jenalee and Noah's eyes to go wide, seeing Trin get along with her mother.

Jenalee rubbed her chin with the back of her left index finger "I'm glad you two are working on this. Still ... The Cross of Sighs was—" Jenalee looked at Jack. "—horrible." Jenalee took a breath. "We've got to think about some way to contain this damn sword. While we're at it, how are we going to contain the whole set—the five artifacts of the Obscurum?"

The question hung over the group like a guillotine blade.

Chapter 37

In her room on board the Helios, Trin called up a number on her cellphone.

Curry answered her cellphone.

"How you doing?"

Curry immediately recognized Trin.

"Trin! It's good to hear you."

"How is Kyle doing?" Trin asked.

"Fragile. He had a lapse like I told you. I'm staying here. I visit every day. I'm keeping my eye on this A-Zone Retreat Center. Some rehab places don't do any good. And some actually cause more damage," Curry said.

"It's good that you're there for him."

"You okay?" Curry asked.

"Long story. You know. Save the world."

"Protect the time-space continuum," Curry said.

"You're not that far off."

"Really?

"Too complicated to go into. I…"

"It's bad. You might not come back?" Curry's voice trembled.

"I'll do my best to come back. You are my family. You and Kyle. I love you two."

"I love you, Trin."

"We can't do better than that."

"You take care of yourself."

"I'll do what's necessary," Trin said.

* * * * * *

Zara, in jaguar form, went full batshit, shark frenzy crazy destroying six punching bags shaped like huge men. Her claws slashed the bags into actual ribbons.

"Having fun?" VoSkhar said, on entering the training room of his estate.

"Never better," she said. "I'm thinking that tearing up Jack AngelSword is going to feel better still."

VoSkhar smiled. He also liked revenge.

Zara's comm device beeped. She listened to a report from a field agent.

Zara looked up at VoSkhar.

"Sir, one of our agents reports that Frederick Asbenrin has been sighted. More than that. Via monitoring devices, we conclude that he has the Judas Gauntlet. Should I take a team and—?" Zara asked.

"No," VoSkhar said. "I'm going to follow your 'slashing model.' That is, I'll take care of Frederick myself."

* * * * * *

After an in-depth conversation in the Ready Room with Mrs. Chi, Jenalee decided to dispatch her team to do some reconnaissance to look for the Judas Gauntlet. According to Mrs. Chi's agents, no one had the Judas Gauntlet yet.

Sahkeisha and Elyse looked into a dealer of antiquities in France.

Trin went on her own to Austria. With her extraordinary skills in both sorcery and martial arts, Jenalee knew Trin could take care of herself.

Jack went with Marta, Trin bristled at that, to Ireland.

Jenalee and Noah went to London. In a sketchy section of town, Jenalee and Noah tracked Dr. Margaret Flax. Jenalee remembered Dr. Flax when she encountered her because Mal had assigned Dr. Flax to study the Flute of Nightmares. Everything about Dr. Margaret Flax gave the impression of a flattened cardboard box. Her vocal tone, her facial expression and her posture.

Jenalee took extra care because Dr. Margaret Flax had seen her face before—when Jenalee and Gram-Gram had retrieved the Flute of Nightmares from her. A stab of grief over Gram-Gram's death hit Jenalee square in the heart. Her chest hurt. She found it hard to breathe.

"Jenalee?" Noah asked.

"I ... I ... I'll be okay."

"Maybe we should abort?" Noah said, concerned.

"No. We go on. This mission—would have been Gram-Gram's mission—if she ... if she were still alive," Jenalee managed to whisper.

Dr. Margaret Flax went into a building. Just then, a guy with two ponytails down to the lower end of his shoulder blades—jumped out the window, escaping having to talk with Dr. Margaret Flax.

Ponytails wore a backpack.

"The way it bounces—that backpack," Noah said.

"He's carrying the Judas Gauntlet," Jenalee said. "We must stop him."

Seeing Jenalee and Noah running toward him, Ponytails ran as if an Olympic starter gun had just gone off.

Desperate to get away, Ponytails ran out of the sketchy neighborhood into a marketplace. He dumped produce, blocking Jenalee. He darted to his left and evaded Noah.

Did we have to get stuck with an Olympic runner? Jenalee

thought.

Ponytails took a left, then a right and another right. He had left Jenalee and Noah far behind.

Ponytails found himself in a dead-end alley. Out of the shadows, VoSkhar stepped forth.

"I'll take that," VoSkhar said.

Ponytails spun on his heel to run the other way.

VoSkhar raised his right hand, sent a bolt of energy, like a hand at Ponytails. The magical hand caught him.

With his left palm, VoSkhar sent another energy-hand to pluck the backpack off Ponytails' back.

Ponytails remained pinned to the ground by the energy-hand issued from VoSkhar's right hand.

"Frederick, I invited you to peacefully come in and give me the Judas Gauntlet. Remember, this is your fault," VoSkhar said as he placed the backpack on his own shoulder.

His left hand now free, VoSkhar had an energy-hand issue from his left palm.

Frederick-Ponytails watched in horror as the energy hand transformed—sort of like a hydra. Instead of multiple heads, the energy hand transformed into twenty hands holding razor-sharp knives.

With a smile, VoSkhar had the knives deliver many cuts.

"Death by—say it,"

Moaning and whimpering, Frederick-Ponytails couldn't speak.

"Say it."

"—thou—sand—cuts."

VoSkhar's smile widened and showed his teeth.

"Precisely."

The twenty-energy-hands reached out and pealed twenty patches of skin off Frederick-Ponytails' body. His screams pierced the quad between buildings.

"Sir," one of VoSkhar's guards said. "Perhaps, we might exit. Local authorities will respond."

"Yes. For now, keeping my personal brand bloodless is appropriate," VoSkhar said.

The energy-hands finished by *pulling apart* Frederick-Ponytails.

Moments later, Jenalee and Noah arrived.

They were careful not to get any of the blood on them—the red liquid disbursed everywhere.

"VoSkhar did this."

"How do you know?" Noah asked.

"I've had some discussions with Mrs. Chi—about VoSkhar and his true form, the demon Khodan."

"Are we sure that this was the guy with the Judas Gauntlet?"

Jenalee pointed.

Noah saw the ripped section of Frederick-Ponytails' face. And his two ponytails nearby.

Chapter 38

"Wrenda ... she was my enemy or my friend," Marta said to Jenalee, as they sat in the Grand Hall.

"Could it be that she changed her perception of you?" Jenalee said.

"I've lived so long. I thought I understood the patterns of life," Marta said.

"Maybe the way to deal with life or existence is—" Jenalee began. "—saying 'I don't know.' That can be the start. It's how to avoid ossifying. Then you're still vibrant and alive."

"That's not helping."

"Oh," Jenalee said. "Maybe I should have done what Noah does?"

"What's that?"

"He just keeps silent until I say something."

Marta laughed, and Jenalee joined her.

Twenty minutes later, Jenalee and her team gathered in the Ready Room on board the Helios.

After Jack and Trin gave their report, Sahkeisha and Elyse communicated that they hadn't found anything.

"We should do some more reconnaissance," Jenalee said to her assembled team—Jack, Noah, Elyse, Sahkeisha, Marta and Trin.

"Isn't that what Mrs. Chi's agents are doing?" Sahkeisha

said. "We already have a good plan."

"I still need more information. I want to see VoSkhar's weaknesses," Jenalee began. "I want to watch how VoSkhar orders his team. How they do his security. See if we can find some team members who resent him—who might hesitate to put their lives on the line."

"That's how I got the sacred text from Mal's estate in Italy. Mal had someone disloyal to him," Jack said.

"When did that happen?" Noah asked.

"At the Tower in Venice, Italy."

A silence came over the room.

Trin looked at the team members.

Jenalee's cellphone buzzed. She looked at a text message.

"We just got word. VoSkhar was sighted near that London marketplace. That confirms what Noah and I surmised. If VoSkhar came out and killed that guy—"

"We thought of him as Ponytails—" Noah said.

"It's likely that VoSkhar had a big reason."

"Probably, VoSkhar took the Judas Gauntlet from him," Jack said.

"We've got to move people," Jenalee said.

Minutes later, Jenalee and her team closed in on the marketplace where one of Mrs. Chi's agents said that she saw VoSkhar.

"There he is," Sahkeisha called over the comm line."

"Let's trail him until he gets to a secluded area—so we can avoid civilians getting stuck in the crossfire," Jenalee said.

About thirty minutes later, VoSkhar walked with three of his guards through a set of abandoned buildings.

"Elyse and Sahkeisha, you take him from the right.

Sahkeisha, use your magic bulbs. Elyse, you handle any thugs near you two. Jack and I can—"

"Roger that," Elyse said.

Sahkeisha and Elyse went on the attack.

VoSkhar turned and used his palms to project two bolts of magical energy. One caught Elyse and the other caught Sahkeisha, tossing them back.

The bolts of energy slammed both Sahkeisha and Elyse into walls. Dazed. Out of the fight.

VoSkhar fired seven magical beams that caused seven balconies to tumble down. Clouds of dust billowed outwards. This afforded VoSkhar and guards a clean getaway.

"Abort," Jenalee said over the comm line. "Recover Sahkeisha and Elyse."

Minutes later, Jenalee and her team members got back on board the Helios. Crew people used stretchers to take Sahkeisha and Elyse to the Healing Center.

Chapter 39

"VoSkhar has both the Cross of Sighs *and* the Judas Gauntlet," Mal said, his large frame dominating his study at his estate.

"So that's the report from your minions?" Hellene said, flapping her wings and moving her perch on Mal's favorite desk.

Mal turned to Sable and said, "Would you get her—it—that thing—out of here?"

"Her name is Hellene. I stay. And she stays," Sable said.

Hellene chucked.

Mal frowned and said, "You're enjoying this too much."

Sable and Hellene shared a look.

"Fine," Mal said. "I was about to suggest that we get ready for a frontal assault to take on VoSkhar at one of his estates. But I remember what you said, Sable. About having leverage and strategy. So, do you have a mole in VoSkhar's circle? And what do you suggest?"

Sable and Hellene shared a look and said together, "He can be taught."

"Enough," Mal said. "After we accomplish this, you two can go on the road with your comedy act."

"The best thing is to think of how we can isolate him," Sable said. "Obviously his home estates will be well defended—each one like a fortress.

"I know that as a fact," Hellene said.

Mal looked at her intently.

"As the head of the House of Dagger, of course, VoSkhar will have the best soldiers to defend him so that he can feel safe at home. However, he also has a big ego," Sable said.

"You know what they say, Big ego, small—" Hellene said.

"Just stay with the plan of attack," Mal said.

"At a conference, he might have to travel through certain hallways—" Sable said.

"Thus, we discover where he will appear. We study the layout of the location and find out where the choke points are," Hellene said.

"Just so," Sable said.

Mal bit his lip and then simply nodded.

Chapter 40

Jenalee knocked on Jack's door.

"Got a couple minutes, Jack?" Jenalee asked.

Opening the door, Jack said, "Certainly."

Jenalee sat down, taking the chair near Jack's desk. "You okay. You've been through so much."

"I'm not sure. I did my training with Shuren Kato."

"How did it go?"

"Good. I think. I faced some stuff," Jack acted quickly to change the subject, "What I don't get is how you forgave Trin so fast to follow her advice—"

"About Shuren Kato?"

Jack nodded.

From her peripheral vision, Jenalee noted a clock—old-fashioned with hands on it.

This reminded her of the clock on Trin's nightstand, in her room.

Trin, Marta and Jenalee sat in chairs near Trin's desk.

"You had another idea?" Jenalee began.

"Why?" Trin asked.

"What?" Jenalee furrowed her eyebrows.

"Why would you listen to me? That fucking demon fooled me like—"

"What is this other idea?" Marta said.

"My martial arts master," Trin said.

163

"Wait a minute—" Jenalee said.

"There is a difference," Trin said.

Jenalee listened.

"My mother knows Master Shuren Kato," Trin said. "They were friends."

"Were?"

"I really don't know the details. I can guess ... And—I was asked to leave Shuren Kato's Academy," Trin said.

"I will go with you to the area near Shuren Kato's Academy. I'll go no further. I will not be welcome," Marta said.

"Why?"

"People judge. In particular, my kind are judged," Marta said.

"I am relying on you—people I don't trust," Jenalee said, eyeing both Trin and Marta.

"I understand why you do not trust me," Trin said. "What has she done? Besides being a vampire."

"Isn't that enough?"

"I warned Jack of The Council's plan," Marta said. "Either the Chest of the House of Dagger had to be destroyed or Jack would have been killed. I warned Jack. I stuck my neck out. And you took action. You eliminated the Chest—and Jack was safe."

"Safe ..."

"At least from The Council."

Jenalee turned to Trin. "How could you ever think that I would trust you when you never trusted Jack? Over and over again, Jack asked you—just about begged you—to let us use the Silent Scepter to save my friends."

"I was on my mission," Trin began. "I accomplished my mission. I have now protected my family. I've killed Uncle Richard, and now no one has a reason to kill my closest friend and her teen brother. How could you expect that I would not do everything I could do to protect my family?"

"Your family? Isn't Mrs. Chi your mother. Isn't she family?"

"How well do you know Mrs. Chi?" Trin asked. "Do you realize what she would give up? You, Jack, me, anybody, and in fact the entire crew of the Helios, to protect what she thinks is the good and the moral and the right of the universe. We are all expendable to my mother."

"I don't know that."

"Trin speaks the truth," Marta said.

"How do you know this?" Trin asked.

"Three reasons. I've been alive for centuries. I know the truth when I hear it. And—I know things because I have sources," Marta said.

"Jenalee?" Jack asked, rousing Jenalee from her memory.

"You want to know how I decided to believe Trin and agree to take you to Shuren Kato?"

Jack nodded.

"We told each other the truth."

Chapter 41

"You forgave Trin," Noah said to Jenalee, as they walked on the SkyLevel.

"How do you know that?" Jenalee asked.

"You forgave her enough to let her be part of this team."

Jenalee nodded. She flexed her right hand and remembered …

Jenalee flexed her right hand. If only it were as easy to drop all the tension she felt about Trin. Would she let Trin help the team? How could she trust Trin?

A knock at her door.

Jenalee welcomed Sahkeisha into her room.

Sahkeisha closed the door behind her. She had an absent thought that the hum of the Helios engines was quieter in the rooms than in the corridor.

"You look serious," Jenalee said.

"Damn right. I've been gearing up to talk with you," Sahkeisha said

"I don't see any new gear," Jenalee said. Her joke fell flat.

"Listen up, girl. This might be the most important thing I say to you ever," Sahkeisha said. "Do I have your attention? You got to let Trin out of the dog house or whatever fucking space, you got her in. She can be an important asset to this team. And you're messing with her head and heart. You know, she's just sick about what happened to Jack. And you know —"

"But—" Jenalee said.

"Just give me a moment to get this out," Sahkeisha said. "You do what you have to do to forgive her to just get your head out of your butt. We need you to lead this team. Now, I was stuck in that coma, so I don't know how you did it. But you somehow carried on with your heart busted to pieces when Gram-Gram died. All right. I'm done. What you got to say?"

Jenalee stood, tears welling up. "I don't know how to do this."

"Then we do it together," Sahkeisha said. "You talk to me. We walk on the SkyLevel. You meditate, do tai chi, yoga. You do what you got to do."

About twenty minutes later, Jenalee went to the SkyLevel and began her run. Moments later, Sahkeisha stepped off the elevator and watched Jenalee run for time.

As Jenalee came close to her, then Sahkeisha ran up to Jenalee's side.

"You're going to have to slow down I was not made for the Olympics," Sahkeisha said.

Jenalee looked at Sahkeisha's mangled left arm, flopping at her side while she ran.

Jenalee felt a stab of pain in her gut. She felt responsible for Sahkeisha losing her life path as a concert pianist. Jenalee thought to herself: I must make better decisions. Some mistakes I cannot afford to make. Otherwise, my friends will pay a horrible price.

Sahkeisha noted Jenalee observing her flopping mangled right arm. "It don't make a pleasing sight, huh? I'd say I got used to it, but that would just be a lie. But I do okay. And so will you, Jenalee."

About an hour later, Jenalee found Daniel and asked, "Did you recover the video footage of Jack and Trin on the tower?"

"Yes. I was going to find you. There is audio, too," Daniel said.

Daniel and Jenalee watched the video monitor. The image

revealed: Daniel's Drone flew up and then hovered about nine feet away from where Jack and Trin confronted each other on the ledge—at the bell tower in Venice, Italy.

"Jack, stay back!" Trin told Jack.

"What's going on?" Jack said.

"It's the Sword—I can't—I—"

"I'll help you," Jack said. "Drop the Sword."

"I can't."

"Maybe my AngelSword can break that Sword."

"Don't try. Stay back," Trin said.

The Sword of the Dark Bloom pulled her forward.

Jack blocked the Sword's strikes. Although Trin swung her arm and the Sword, her face revealed her reluctance.

Jack saw Trin's eyes, wide, horrified.

Jack missed a block. The Sword plunged into Jack's gut.

"Jack! I didn't mean to—"

The AngelSword touched the Sword of the Dark Bloom. Jack saw his arm thrust forward. The AngelSword sliced deep into Trin's gut.

"No!" Jack grunted.

Energy emanated from Jack and Trin connected by the swords. An arch of the energy aimed at the drone. The image winked out. Apparently, the energy struck the drone and damaged it.

Daniel looked away from the monitor. He saw Jenalee frown and take in a big breath.

Thirty minutes after her conversation with Daniel, Jenalee found Trin at the Grand Hall. Trin looked out the window watching the passing clouds.

"I misjudged you," Jenalee said. "—and for that ... please forgive me. "

"You're asking me to—?" Trin said.

"I realize now that I was screwed up inside," Jenalee began. "I just hated myself. And it had nothing to do with you. Maybe a bit

had something to do with you."

Jenalee and Trin share a rueful smile.

"But the point is that I felt that I failed to protect my grandmother," Jenalee said. "On some level, I realized that even in your fighting with Jack—those many times—you were trying to protect him. Because obviously you're a better warrior than Jack is."

Trin listened.

"What happened? What caused you to stab Jack?" Jenalee asked.

"I saw some energy—some essence of—I'm thinking that it was my Uncle Richard," Trin began. "I think Uncle Richard pushed my arm. Uncle Richard still wants to hurt me. And I'm thinking Uncle Richard pressed Jack's arm to have the AngelSword strike me. That's how we both went to the Ethereal Plane."

"You okay, Jenalee?" Noah asked.

"I'm okay. Just thinking about something Sahkeisha said about forgiving," Jenalee said.

"You know what is unforgivable?" Noah said. "It is what is in us that we see in another. That dark smear that is in us—that we cannot forgive. What can't you forgive, Jenalee?"

Jenalee looked away. She whispered, "I didn't protect Gram-Gram."

Noah remained silent.

"Go on. Say what you're thinking," Jenalee said.

"So, you lead us out of duty and obligation to the memory of Gram-Gram?"

"What's wrong with that?"

"Is that enough?" Noah asked.

"What more could there be?"

"You tell me," Noah said.

"And who made you my shrink, anyway?"

Noah got to his feet. He stepped forward, toward the elevator door of the SkyLevel.

"Where're you going?" Jenalee said.

"I thought you seemed to need some alone-time—" Noah said.

"Maybe, I do," Jenalee said sharply.

Chapter 42

I just reran the words Noah and I had talked about. As I walked along the path in Mrs. Chi's Animal Sanctuary. I was grateful to be outside. This pitstop for the Helios was an opportunity for me to see some scenery and walk alone. Time to think. Time to feel.

"You know what is unforgivable? It is what is in us that we see in another. That dark smear that is in us—that we cannot forgive. What can't you forgive, Jenalee?" Noah asked.

"I didn't protect Gram-Gram." I said.

"So, you lead us out of duty and obligation to the memory of Gram-Gram?" Noah asked.

I keep rerunning that the thought: "I didn't ask for this."

I just wanted to explore my possibilities at college. I hadn't declared any major. It was just my first year of college. First year? Just a couple of months. And here I am.

Where is here?

I mean, inside me. My heart.

Did I mean it about how Daniel had the answer? Just go back to college.

Mrs. Chi would get someone else to save the world—or the 9 Realms

Besides, I already had a role. In about two years and a few months, I will have to do my duty as the Gate Guardian. I made that promise to Gram-Gram.

What if I die before I must do my duties as the Gate Guardian?

No, it's not that—

Whump! I found myself on my butt.

I looked around. Then realized that I had been so stuck in my own thoughts that I had missed an irregularity in the cement of the path. I had tripped and paid for it with the pain in my backside.

Nobody was around.

Fine! I'll just sit here.

I actually had a new point of view. I could see through a gap in the foliage. A bear reached for food, and another bear went for it.

With a mighty roar and a sweep of a claw, the initial bear made the interloper back off. She then took the food with her—to an area fifteen feet away—where a couple of bear cups tumbled together, playing. She placed the food in front of the bear cubs. They stopped playing and dived in for their meal.

This bear. She was both warrior and mother and …

The ideas tumbled together in my mind. Duty. Warrior. Mother. Love. She was both.

The ideas formed into a different perception.

I begin with my grief of losing Gram-Gram.

I lead the team because of duty and obligation.

Was there a way for me to do "both this and that"?

The mother bear—at least in the wild—will have to face her cubs growing up and leaving.

But my problem was not forgiving myself for making mistakes. Sending my people into situations that … I'm going to lose someone. Not like Daniel. He's safe.

I'm going *to lose someone to death.*

Gram-Gram had encouraged me to not get tangled up in

my thinking. She often said, *Show up to each moment fresh.*

I don't know if I can do that. Maybe I'm supposed to make decisions and ... realize I don't control much. And I'll need to be okay with that.

* * * * * *

Wham—Jenalee heard an explosive sound rising from the Adversary Room on board the Helios.

She came around the corner and entered the room. On the floor, she saw four demolished punching bags. Marta did a kick to a fifth bag, which split in half as if she had kicked tissue paper.

"Looks like Mrs. Chi is going to send a crew member to order and pick up a bunch more punching bags," Jenalee said.

"I'll have to apologize to her and give her the funds to cover these casualties," Marta said.

"Seems like you got past the depressed part and now you're in the rage part."

"Part of what?" Marta said.

"Grief."

Marta turned away. "I don't know if Wrenda was ever really my friend. The last thing she said to me is: 'When you know, please forgive me.'"

Marta kicked one of the sections of a punching bag across the room. "How can I ever forgive her? She took from me... She turned me into a raging monster who destroyed my husband. I can never forget the look in Ethan's eyes when the Madness had me tear off his arm. The hurt. The betrayal. Wrenda caused that."

Jenalee remained silent.

Marta continued, "But the recent ten years ... I mean, I

was there for her when she lost her goddaughter. And Wrenda was there for me during my fears, my disappointments. I looked at her closet. She had kept every blouse that I had bought for her birthday. All ten of them."

Marta shook her head. "And I saw her eyes just before she died. It was genuine. She had genuine regret that she had ever caused me to lose my husband, Ethan. We were only going to have a few more years. I mean, to a vampire, human lives are just so short."

Marta's fist closed and started to shake with her rage.

Jenalee tossed half a punching bag at Marta. With Marta's punch, the bag disintegrated.

"Causing me to kill my dear husband, Ethan. It's searing pain that I carry millennium after Millennium. As long as I exist, this pain, this loss of Ethan, is something I carry."

Marta looked at Jenalee. "I don't know why I'm telling you all this. Maybe it's because I heard that you lost your grandmother recently. So you understand."

Jenalee nodded.

Marta looked off in the distance. "I don't have the words to tell you how it's seared my heart when I recovered from the Madness. To know that I destroyed Ethan. It was only one thing that stopped me from just killing myself. It was a promise."

Jenalee whispered, "A promise..."

"To Ethan," Marta began. "Ethan accepted my nature. He knew that I would outlive him. It was strange ..." A tear went down Marta's face.

Hundreds of years earlier. Marta looked up to see rainwater dripping into their small home.

Ethan said, "I know you. When I die it's going to knock you down. So, I want you to promise me that for at least one year after my death, you will find something or some cause or someone to help ... to support. You know, I believe in our colonies and our need to free ourselves from the King's tyranny."

Marta nodded.

"You need to ... I'm asking you to look for something to support or someone to support. I want you to carry on. Because of your nature, you can provide a continuity. I'm just going to be here like a brief candle. But you—you're like the ocean ever flowing, ever-renewing. You can be a force of nature. A force for continued good."

In the present, Marta felt tears streaming down her face. She wiped them and took a big breath. "I don't know if I can ever forgive Wrenda."

"Is there some part of you that wants to?" Jenalee asked.

Marta gave the slightest of nods.

"Maybe that's enough."

Chapter 43

Trin, Marta, Jenalee, Jack and Noah gathered in a hotel room near the Conference Convention Center that VoSkhar had scheduled to give his presentation.

"So, you all have your assignments," Jenalee said. "With four branches of tunnels below the convention center, the main point is to cut off a number of VoSkhar's guards so that we can take him."

"If we take him, we still have the problem. He may not have the Cross of Sighs and the Judas Gauntlet on him," Jack said.

"Even in his disguise as Master Haito, I noticed that VoSkhar had a habit. He would carry his most precious items. It seems that when something is important to him, he won't leave it, perhaps, in a vault that could be breached while he's not on the premises. Maybe he thinks that he is so powerful that he has no worries," Trin said.

"He *is* damn powerful," Marta said.

"We'll have to hope that we can use a surprise attack," Jenalee said.

Thirty minutes later, Sahkeisha and Elyse held their position at the East branch of the underground tunnels.

"You'll tell me if you think any action is a stupid way to die," Sahkeisha said.

"Sure, I'll tell you if it's a tossed salad,"

"Tuna salad," Sahkeisha said. Elyse gave her a kiss on her cheek.

"North branch is quiet," Marta confirmed.

"South branch all clear," Trin said.

Standing next to Jenalee at the West branch of the tunnels, both Noah and Jack fidgeted like racehorses before a race.

Marta reported on her comm line, "I've just seen Mal Pala, and he's with a woman."

"Describe her," Jenalee said.

"Tall. Looks like a model. Has blond hair."

"Shit. It's Sable Cane. Could it be that Mal has released her from the InBetween?" Jenalee said.

Noah nodded in sympathy to Jenalee.

"Marta, keep surveillance on the two, but do not engage."

"Damn right. Do not engage," Trin said. "You got two sorcery types. Too much for one vampire."

"Not just any vampire."

"Fine. You're special," Trin said. "Still, Mal and Sable Cane—they have strong magical capabilities."

Marta sighed. "I will not engage."

Sahkeisha said, "We're seeing VoSkhar over here. He has six guards. Wait a minute."

"What's going on?" Jenalee said.

Sahkeisha continued. "One guard stopped. VoSkhar bumped into him. He dropped his briefcase. It opened. Just before VoSkhar slammed it shut—I saw two items in the briefcase—"

"Are they—?"

"Yes. Judas Gauntlet and the Cross of Sighs."

Just then, Jenalee's team heard the roar of explosions.

Mal Pala and Sable blasted VoSkhar's guards. Screams. Shouts. Chaos.

Elyse said, "This is our chance to get that briefcase. We've got to get the artifacts. We can't let them fall into the hands of Mal."

"Wait for us to get there," Trin said. "VoSkhar is too strong."

"I'll make a distraction so Sahkeisha can use her magic bulbs—and tangle VoSkhar in her magical vines," Elyse said. "When he is immobilized, I'll get the briefcase."

"No, this won't work," Trin said.

Jack looked at Jenalee. This was her call.

Jenalee said, "Sahkeisha, you tell me: Is this tuna salad? Is this a stupid way—"

"No risk, no reward. We'll do it. All right?" Sahkeisha asked.

"Go ahead. Be careful."

Elyse got ahead of Sahkeisha and went to the right—some distance from VoSkhar. Using her baton, Elyse took out a couple of guards. She made sure to make lots of noise, and true to form, VoSkhar was distracted.

Sahkeisha threw five magical bulbs, causing vines to manifest and tangle up VoSkhar. The vines also caused havoc among VoSkhar's closest guards.

Elyse ran in and grabbed the briefcase and tossed it to Sahkeisha. VoSkhar sent out bolts of energy—two struck Elyse and Sahkeisha. Both hit opposing walls. The collision broke Sahkeisha's one functional arm. The briefcase fell and opened on impact.

The Cross of Sighs and the Judas Gauntlet tumbled out.

At that moment, Mal and Sable charged into the area from the North branch.

They ignored Sahkeisha grimacing on the floor. Elyse remained unmoving in a corner.

Jack and Jenalee arrived while bolts of energy were flying

back and forth between VoSkhar, Sable and Mal.

Having worked himself free of Sahkeisha's tangle-vines, VoSkhar got hold of the Judas Gauntlet. He turned to reach for the Cross of Sighs, but Sable hit him with a bolt of energy. VoSkhar tumbled, knocked back eleven feet.

Mal tossed a bag onto the Cross of Sighs and used the bag as a barrier between his skin and the artifact. Stuck in the bag, the Cross of Sighs squirmed like a trapped rattlesnake.

Due to the previous explosions and various bolts of energy causing damage, the ceiling overhead began to buckle.

"Retreat," Jenalee called.

Using their combined bolts of energy, Mal and Sable blasted a hole to the street level. They dashed away.

Still clutching the Judas Gauntlet, VoSkhar cast a spell to give himself a forcefield to protect him from the collapsing structure.

Jenalee and Jack grabbed Sahkeisha. Noah and Marta reached for Elyse, still unconscious. Marta pulled Elyse away from Noah, as she found it easier to carry Elyse in a bridal carry by herself.

The overhead structure continued to give way.

Jenalee choked on the dust rising. *Have I made the wrong call again? Is my team going to die in this rubble?*

Chapter 44

Safe in his energy forcefield, VoSkhar looked about. The network of tunnels below the conference area had filled in for the most part. The collapse of supports and the dust gave him the impression that Jenalee and her team had perished. He smiled.

As the rumbling sounds died down, VoSkhar moved under one standing support beam. He placed the Judas Gauntlet inside his shirt next to his chest. He aimed his hand upward with a magical spell to drill a hole to the street level.

Feeling the fresh air rush from the hole, VoSkhar aimed his hands downward and use his magical force beams to propel himself upward and out of the hole. He left the area.

Some feet away, Jenalee and team members continued coughing, while they waited for the Helios to send down its elevator.

Catching her breath, Jenalee said, "The balance of power has changed. Mal has the fourth artifact, the Cross of Sighs. But VoSkhar retains the Judas Gauntlet."

The Helios extraction team helped Jenalee and her teams get the badly injured Sahkeisha and Elyse to the Healing Center.

After talking with Mrs. Chi's medical personnel, Jenalee felt assured that her friends would start to recover. Mrs. Chi did a spell to aid in the healing of Sahkeisha's right arm. Jenalee looked on knowing that her own knowledge of healing spells was not much in comparison.

Unfortunately, both Sahkeisha and Elyse would be sidelined for the next assignments in the field.

At the Grand Hall, Jenalee took sips of hot chocolate in a cup that warmed her hands. *How did I make this wrong call?* she thought. Her heart felt broken. *I did this. I didn't stick with the plan. Almost took away Sahkeisha's music—her right arm broken. And almost took Sahkeisha's life. And Elyse almost died, too. My fault. I did this,*

She got up and took the elevator. She ended up in a secluded corner of the SkyLevel.

Noah approached slowly.

"That's it. I'm done," Jenalee said.

"Done with what?" Noah asked.

"Done. I quit."

Jenalee got up and went toward the elevator door.

"Where're you going?" Noah asked.

"To Mrs. Chi. She can drop me off at college. Daniel had the right idea. I'm only goddamn eighteen years old. What do I know about leading a team to stop some asshole from changing reality? Have you looked around? Maybe reality needs changing,"

Noah listened.

"You're doing that thing again."

"What?" he asked.

"Letting me talk. Letting me flail about."

"You want something else?"

"An answer! A goddamn answer!"

"What was the question?"

"Why won't Mrs. Chi leave me alone? Pick someone else. Fucking shit! She's been doing this for decades. She found other teams. Sent other soldiers in. Nothing says I have to be the patsy. The dumbass who … who screws it all up."

Noah listened.

Jenalee glared. She looked him straight in the eye.

"Say something. And it better be good," Jenalee said.

Noah took a couple of deep breaths. "You're called, Jenalee. Answer the call. Don't answer the call. You choose. Whatever you do, I'll back you up," Noah said.

"You would?"

"You know I would." He opened his arms and Jenalee hugged him fiercely.

"You're important to me. I have a question," Noah said.

"I don't know if I'm up to this," Jenalee said. "... All right. Let's put it all on the table. What's the question?" Jenalee said.

"Maybe you're just tired. You don't have enough energy."

"That's not a question. It's true but it's not a question."

"Not having energy is not just about running after our ... opponents and being physically tired. So ... here's the question. What's really bothering you—what's draining your energy? Noah asked.

"I don't know. I keep doing what I'm supposed to do. But I don't ... I don't know," Jenalee said.

"Okay. How about we just sit here a while?"

Some minutes later, Jenalee said again, "I made the wrong call ... I had a feeling. But what was the source of the feeling?"

"What were you thinking?" Noah asked.

"I was afraid that we'd lose this one chance. VoSkhar would get away with Judas Gauntlet."

"How did you know this?"

"I—I was thinking. I was afraid ...so that's about fear."

"Maybe the question is: What is the source of the feeling—fear or intuition?"

"But how would I know—in the particular moment?" Jenalee asked.

"Where do you feel something you know to be true?"

"Like what?"

"Where do you feel your love for Gram-Gram?"

Jenalee took a deep breath. "I feel ... I feel it in my heart. It feels warm."

"Where did you feel things when you made the call?—for us to skip the plan and send Sahkeisha and Elyse in on the right flank?"

"It was—it is. I can feel it come back. It is high up in my chest. Like near my collar bone. A bit hard to breathe. Discomfort."

Noah remained silent.

"There *is* a difference," Jenalee said. "Are you telling me just notice where I feel it in my body? That's how I'm going to make the right call?"

Noah leaned back onto the backrest of the bench. He paused.

"I've been studying about this," Noah began. "There's some research, some discussion about this. The idea is to observe yourself. Each individual is different," Noah said.

* * * * * *

Mrs. Chi called Jenalee to her Ready Room of the Helios.

"Because Sable Cane escaped the InBetween," Mrs. Chi began. "—I have agents guarding Daniel. He has *not* been approached."

Jenalee sunk into a chair.

"You must prepare."

"I'll go to the Adversary Room now," Jenalee said.

"That is only part of your preparation."

Jenalee recalled something she read. Someone named Stephen Ramsey said, "In times of stress, we revert to our preparation."

"You must outplan, outthink, outprepare your opponent," Mrs. Chi said.

"I will be in the library."

Jenalee rose, bowed to Mrs. Chi and left.

"Miyamoto Musashi?" Noah asked, on finding Jenalee reading a book about the legendary swordsman.

"More military strategy. I was never interested in this stuff, but you do what you have to," Jenalee said.

"So, what have you found?"

"Miyamoto Musashi wrote, 'You must understand that there is more than one path to the top of the mountain.' …"

"You just brightened up. What's going on?" Noah said.

"I just got an idea. I just used a Musashi idea as a springboard in my thinking," Jenalee said. She pointed to a page in the book. "It says here "Know your enemy, know his sword."

Jenalee rose to her feet. "Come with me to the Adversary Room. I've got to practice. I'm going to fight Sable—but not in the way she expects. I'm going to deny her the use of her sword."

"What does that mean?"

"I'll show you."

Chapter 45

"I've given this a lot of thought. I've already said the plan is to get Mal to fight VoSkhar and so the two of them will either destroy each other or weaken each other," Jenalee said to the assembled Jack, Trin, Mrs. Chi, Marta, and Noah in the Ready Room.

"Logical and well thought out," Mrs. Chi said.

"Again, it's my studies," Jenalee said. "Sun Tzu wrote 'The supreme art of war is to subdue the enemy without fighting.'"

"I don't know how you intend to control VoSkhar and Mal—and now we know that Sable Cane is in the mix," Noah said.

"We must force them to appear someplace," Jenalee said.

"How can we do that?" Jack asked.

"We *did* get Trin to show up at the cemetery for her father's ashes," Jenalee said.

Trin frowned. "So you say we trick them?"

"Exactly," Jenalee said. "What will get them both to show up?"

"A chance to possess all five of the Obscurum artifacts," Marta said.

"We need something more than that," Jenalee said.

"Really?" Noah asked. "What could they possibly want more?"

"At any time, they will raid the other for the artifacts that they don't have," Mrs. Chi said.

"So, we control that," Jenalee said.

"How?" Jack asked.

"We make them think they need something else. So, I'm asking all of us here to think of what we could do about that," Jenalee said.

They were quiet for a time. Thinking.

"We could make them think that there is a sixth element to the Obscurum," Trin said.

"Good. I agree," Jenalee said.

"But everyone has been studying every sacred text," Jack said. "It's not like we can just put out an article on the Internet and—"

"Why not? People believe in fake news all the time. The stupid bastards," Noah said.

"But we're not dealing with idiots," Trin said. "The source of the news would have to be unimpeachable."

"There's no one like that … I mean … except Dr. Lara Authyn," Jack said.

"Who?" Jenalee asked.

"She's an incredible scholar and researcher. And she was my mentor—when I earned my Ph.D.," Jack said.

"Then we have you get her to release the news," Jenalee said.

"No. She … she has cancer. She won't want to have her legacy be that she lied or that she was fooled," Jack said.

"She trusts you, right?" Jenalee asked.

"Yes—because I've never shaken up her worldview. She was my *mentor*. I don't see how we convince her to release any news that would tarnish her legacy."

"Then we find a way," Jenalee said.

Jack stood in Dr. Lara Authyn's classroom. Jack knew her

habit of being in her classroom to think and plan her next day's class. Dr. Lara rolled her wheelchair to jot certain notes on the whiteboards.

At 8 pm, no students were in the room.

"So that's the situation," Jack said, in a summary of presenting the situation that Jenalee and her team faced.

"You expect me to believe that the ideas are true?" Dr. Lara asked. "The Obscurum can actually change reality. You know I'm an atheist. None of the religious pablum means anything to me."

"I had a feeling that something else would be required," Jack said. "Dr. Lara, I'd like to introduce you to some friends of mine." Jack pressed a device in his right ear—his comm line. "Please join us."

Jenalee opened the classroom door. Then, she, Marta, Trin and Noah stepped inside.

Once the door was shut, Trin held up her palms. Energy and fire roared between them.

"Impressive. A great illusion. Stage magic." Dr. Lara said.

Marta said, "Understandable. Allow me to join in."

Marta moved at vampire-speed to stand next to Dr. Lara. Marta's movement fluttered Dr. Lara's hair. She was startled.

Then, Marta smiled, and her incisor teeth elongated. Marta darted at vampire-speed over to Noah, and, using one hand, she picked him up over her head.

"Hey!" Noah said.

Marta held Noah aloft with evident ease.

Impressed, Dr. Lara leaned back in her wheelchair.

* * * * * *

"Where is Mal Pala?" VoSkhar said, through gritted teeth.

"Our agents have not found him. He's off the grid," jaguar-Zara said as she prowled in VoSkhar's study at his estate.

"Our best move is to pounce on him when he's not looking," VoSkhar said.

"I like that word *pounce*," jaguar-Zara said, flexing her claws in her right paw.

"Thought you would."

VoSkhar took a breath. Then his form shifted. In his demon-Khodan-form, he smiled. His razor-sharp teeth gleamed in the low light.

As a reflex, jaguar-Zara also smiled revealing her vicious teeth.

"We must be ready. A multi-layered plan. I have the sense that Jenalee Storm and her team will be close by," Khodan-VoSkhar said.

"Where Jenalee is, Jack AngelSword will be near. He is mine," jaguar-Zara said.

"Of course."

"I can just taste Jack's blood—when I have his neck in my jaws, and I snap it," jaguar-Zara said. "I will avenge my brother. And Jack will die in the most excruciating way possible."

Chapter 46

"Wow. What a cynic," Jenalee said to Jack—while Marta, Noah, Trin and Mrs. Chi settled in their chairs of the Ready Room.

"Not cynic," Jack said. "Skeptic. I've always know Dr. Lara to be skeptical."

"You know, it's said that a cynic is a disillusioned idealist," Trin said.

Jack shook his head. "I didn't know that Dr. Lara had a price."

Jack went silent.

"You look disillusioned, Jack," Marta said. "It was what she wanted."

Mrs. Chi's eyes widened as she realized. "You made her a vampire." It was not a question. It was Mrs. Chi's conclusion.

Marta nodded, solemnly.

"What else would a scholar want? More time to learn and know the unknowable," Trin said. "Of course, she's going to keep up the illusion that she needs that wheelchair."

"So, she will leak the idea that there is a sixth artifact that is required for the Obscurum?" Mrs. Chi asked.

Jenalee nodded. "We still need to get VoSkhar, Mal Pala and Sable Cane to be someplace at the same time."

"I can help with that," Mrs. Chi said. "All three are evil. They would only really understand greed and fear. I have a friend Antoine Ahlmain. We can leak the news that he has the sixth artifact. He's so rich, he could have paid some extraordinary price for it. And he is willing to sell it."

"But how could anyone be willing to sell something so evil, so powerful?" Noah asked.

"Greed. He will sell it to the highest bidder," Mrs. Chi said.

"But it still doesn't make sense," Jenalee said. "What is the use of money when the whole world would be twisted and basically destroyed?"

"My friend, Antoine, is a truly vocal atheist. Of course, the artifact is just an object. With legends told about it. Nothing more. To him," Mrs. Chi said.

"I understand," Jack said. "If you don't think the world can be destroyed by a thing—you don't care."

"Antoine does care about something," Mrs. Chi said. "Something important. Friendship. He will do me this favor. But we must keep him safe."

"With VoSkhar, Mal, and Sable around, how could it be possible to keep anybody safe?" Noah asked.

The question reverberated in the Ready Room.

Chapter 47

The night before the scheduled appointment with Antoine that was sure to bring out VoSkhar and Mal Pala, Jenalee assembled her team of Jack, Trin, Noah and Marta. Sahkeisha and Elyse continued to recover, but they remained in the Healing Center.

Jenalee said, "Noah brought this quote to me. He woke me up. I'm looking to be a better leader."

She handed the quote to Noah. "How about you share it, Noah?"

"'Some mistakes will be made along the way, and that's good. Because at least some decisions are being made along the way. And we'll find the mistakes; we'll fix them.' Steve Jobs said that," Noah said.

"So, we're going into battle again," Jenalee began. "Let's talk about our previous battle experiences. Now is the time that we find mistakes, and we fix them."

They talked for a time about past errors in other battles.

Noah said, "Jenalee, I appreciate it when you tell us what is working. That's a good leader. I remember a friend who went into the Army, and he told me about this Captain Roy. He wasn't a good leader. He made them run extra in the morning so they had to choose between breakfast or a shower. Starve or feel sticky all day. One sergeant called the cadence while they were running:

"*I want to eat,*

But he won't quit.
Captain Roy is
Full of shit!"

Jenalee, Noah, Jack, Trin and Marta laughed.

After a couple of moments, Jack stood up. "I have to confront Zara," Jack said to Jenalee, Trin and Marta.

"Why you? And why now?" Jenalee asked.

"Because we have to take out Zara. Like a chess piece, we get her off the board. VoSkhar relies on her. I can't do any good for this team if this raving jaguar-person is going to strike me down when she gets the chance," Jack said.

Jenalee sighed. "I got you into this. Thanks again for taking out Erik. That werewolf would have never stopped until I was in pieces."

"Mrs. Chi said that Zara was spotted at the Bright Star Hotel," Jack said.

"Those have separate bungalows," Trin said, looking up from a laptop screen.

"So, I'll confront her," Jack said.

"All right," Jenalee said, not keen on this plan. "Be sure to take backup."

"I was hoping we could somehow resolve this," Jack said, as he confronted Zara at her bungalow at the Bright Star Hotel.

"We resolve this with your death," Zara said.

Zara moved swiftly and tossed an Aren Shroud onto Jack's arm. This surprised Jack. He didn't know that more than one Shroud existed. The Aren Shroud grabbed Jack's arm like shrink-wrap. The AngelSword winked out of existence.

Zara changed form into a vicious jaguar.

Jaguar-Zara leapt and tossed Jack aside, slamming him

into a wall.

"I'm not going to kill you quick, Jack. You may have killed my brother, Erik, with one slice of your sword. Not me. I'm going to break your bones. All of them. Make you scream for mercy," jaguar-Zara said.

As he staggered, Jack hit a table and knocked the Sword of the Dark Bloom off. The hilt of the sword caught. Two inches of the bland were now visible.

Taking advantage of the opening, the non-corporeal form of Uncle Richard rose from the Sword—as if he was ghastly mist.

Uncle Richard darted over to Jack, enveloped him. Jack felt compelled to draw the Sword of the Dark Bloom from its scabbard.

"Back together again, Jack," Uncle Richard said. "Last time, I made you stab Trin. What will I do with you this time?" He smiled. "Get angry, Jack. Go ahead release your rage."

Jack thought, *Breathe deep. Calm. In … out. I am more than the pain. I am more than anger. Breathe.* Jack held still. Last time, when the Cross of Sighs had it sway with Jack, he had gone berserk, tearing his way through twenty people. This time, using the meditative practices under Shuren Kato's tutelage, Jack held still.

Looking from outside the window of the bungalow, Marta glanced at Jack with the Sword of the Dark Bloom in his hand. Would Jack stay calm? And if so was he impaired? Would he be easy-pickings for jaguar-Zara?

Marta moved like a flash of lightning and grabbed the Sword from Jack, releasing him from the double-grip of Sword and Uncle Richard.

Marta swung the Sword of the Dark Bloom and cut jaguar-Zara in half. Dead—Zara reverted to human form.

The Sword-Demon jumped out of the Sword and plucked the weapon from Marta's hand.

The entity, white hair and eyes ablaze, rammed the Sword through Marta's abdomen. "You draw blood, I draw blood," the Sword Demon said.

Running in from a backroom, Trin, using a spell that she practiced in the Adversary Room, aimed a bolt of magical energy out of her left palm. The bolt caught the Sword Demon, making it freeze.

Jack saw Trin's action.

"I'm sorry," Jack said to Marta. He yanked the Sword out of her abdomen. Marta grunted in agony.

Trin, via her energy bolt, shoved the Sword Demon into Sword's blade.

Trin tossed another bolt of energy at Uncle Richard which caught the non-corporeal entity and shoved him into the Sword's blade.

"Jack, the scabbard," Trin said.

Jack sheathed the Sword into its scabbard. Trin took hold of the Sword.

Jack darted over, grabbed the top half of Zara and shoved Zara's neck near Marta's face.

"Have a drink," Jack said.

Marta sunk her elongated incisor teeth into Zara's neck. She took a deep drink of Zara's remaining blood.

Jack watched. His eyes widened as he saw the wound in Marta's abdomen closing.

Chapter 48

After devoting some time with Marta at the Helios Healing Center, Jack retreated to the SkyLevel. He found the scent of the trees to be calming.

Trin found Jack sitting on a bench.

He looked up at her.

"Need some quiet time alone?" she asked.

"No. I'm good," Jack said, as he gestured that she join him.

"We didn't get the chance to talk about what happened," Trin said.

"Oh, you mean about when we stabbed each other?" Jack said.

"Doesn't quite make for good dinner conversation," Trin said.

"It seems like you came back from the Ethereal Plane changed," Jack began. "You're getting along with your mother. Even Jenalee seems to be okay with you now."

"Now that's the miracle!" Trin said. She and Jack chuckled over that.

Trin looked Jack in the eye. "Changed. Yes. That's true. Before I went to the Ethereal Plane, I thought I knew my purpose. Just protect my family."

"Curry and her teen brother—"

"Kyle. Yes. It was clear. My mother was always 'big picture.' She wouldn't slow down and protect just two people," Trin said. "I'm sorry, Jack, that I didn't find a way to share the Silent Scepter before—when you and Jenalee needed it."

Jack nodded.

"After my experience in the Ethereal Plane, things look different. It was like my purpose of just protecting Curry and Kyle was like a toothpick. And now, I'm meant to be part of something like a mighty redwood tree. I'm sad that your journey to the Ethereal Plane proved so different," Trin said.

"I don't even know if I went to the Ethereal Plane," Jack began. "I do know that I went to the depths. Your Uncle Richard was there. In the depths, I found that the source of my rage—it's always been fear."

Trin reached for Jack's hand. "There something beyond fear, Jack. There are times when only love from others can bring you out of the abyss."

Jack welcomed the hug from Trin.

When the hug was done, Jack looked in Trin's eyes. "I'm glad that you're going to be using the plan to be off VoSkhar's radar."

"Jenalee had a good point that VoSkhar would first look to take me out of the fight," Trin said.

"Stay safe," Jack said.

* * * * * *

"Are you sure the Tahchai Cloaking Spells will conceal us?" Jenalee said over the comm line. She and her team members Marta, Jack, Noah and Trin were hidden in various locations around the abandoned factory where Antoine would face Mal, Sable and VoSkhar. Jenalee was surprised how near this factory stood to the Patriot Hill town square.

Maybe the factory's fumes convinced the leadership of this town to require that this facility close. Perhaps, fumes would drift over the town square.

Jenalee continued, "If I were VoSkhar or his opponents, I would be certain to scan the area—using magic or something else."

"I'm sure the Tahchai Cloaking Spells will work. My mother is good at making stuff like this," Trin said.

"Are we going to see both sides arrive with armies?" Noah asked.

"Unlikely. I've seen, over the centuries, big egos like VoSkhar, Mal and Sable..." Marta began. "These are people who believe that they're so strong that they often choose to just bring a few guards to serve as distractions,"

"That remains to be seen," Jack said.

In a central courtyard, in the shade under a balcony, Antoine stepped out.

"You might as well show yourselves," Antoine said.

VoSkhar, Mal and finally Sable stepped forward, from their places of concealment.

VoSkhar had six guards with him—six guards that were visible.

"Bring out the sixth part of the Obscurum and let's get this over with," Mal said.

"You expect me to hold an auction now for this sixth element?" Antoine asked.

"Probably," VoSkhar said.

"You will be disappointed," Antoine said.

"I am weary of this circus," Mal said, and he sent a bolt of energy at Antoine.

The image of Antoine flickered.

"A hologram," Sable Cane said.

The voice of Antoine grew more pervasive in the area.

"There is no sixth artifact. In fact, there is but one thing more to do. VoSkhar, Mal Pala and Sable Crane—I do hope you enjoy fighting over the set of Obscurum artifacts. Let this be your final battleground."

The transmission of Antoine's voice ended.

VoSkhar, Mal and Sable all moved fast to duck behind various forms of cover.

"You know, we could come to some kind of arrangement," VoSkhar called out from behind some machinery.

"Really?" Mal called back.

"Surely, we all want different things," VoSkhar said.

"And in what order would we use the Obscurum?" Sable said. "Our desires may conflict. The second to use the Obscurum might cancel the changes wrought be the first to employ the instrument."

"A good word 'wrought,'" VoSkhar said. He surreptitiously gestured with his hand that his six soldiers disperse.

"I have no need or use for your praise, and—" Sable said, as she noticed some movement of VoSkhar's personnel.

Sable fired off magical bolts that cut the soldiers down where they stood.

With all six soldiers dead, Sable said, "And, evidently, you had no use for your six soldiers—"

Using his dead personnel as a distraction, VoSkhar had changed his position and sent bolts of energy toward Mal and Sable. One hit a tree branch, pulverizing a section, and the rest of the limb fell and clipped Sable on the leg as she darted to the side.

VoSkhar's next bolt severed half of Mal's left hand, leaving him with two fingers and his thumb. The bolt instantly cauterized Mal's wound.

VoSkhar used this moment to retreat. *I need more pieces on the table to run interference for me,* he thought.

Chapter 49

"Where is he?" Sable asked, looking to locate VoSkhar.

"Don't know," Mal said.

"Your hand!" Sable said, concern in her voice.

"It's cauterized. Let's keep our eye on the ball," Mal said.

Sable could tell that Mal was purposely keeping his voice neutral even though the pain must have been great. Macho, yes. But admirable in a way.

Mal continued to scan the area, glancing about. "There!" He saw someone with the same walking gait as VoSkhar—about one block away.

"He's going to the town square," Sable said.

Mal started to run.

"Hold up. Conserve your energy. We'll walk," Sable said.

Mal looked at her.

"Okay. Briskly."

Mal managed a smile, although his eyes betrayed some wincing with pain.

From her place of concealment, Jenalee said over the comm device, "It's working. Mal's been injured. And all three of them have expelled a lot of energy."

"That confirms it," Jack said.

"What?" Jenalee asked.

"Something I was surmising. These sorcerers expel energy, and there's a limit to their capacity."

"Yes, that's how it works," Trin said over the comm.

"Are you in place, Trin?" Jenalee asked.

"I am."

VoSkhar arrived at the town square. Men, women and children milled about going from shop to shop. Some gazing on two large statues on pedestals—Benjamin Franklin and Thomas Jefferson.

Patriot's Hill. *These bystanders will die for me on this hill,* VoSkhar thought. *Sable and Mal will be here soon. I need a plan for—*

A magical bolt just missed VoSkhar, and he put up a magical shield to block Sable's next strike.

From another direction, a magical bolt struck the balcony over VoSkhar's head. VoSkhar just barely managed to retreat into the recessed doorway of a shop to save himself. The balcony crashed onto the sidewalk where VoSkhar had been a moment before.

Getting out of the doorway, VoSkhar did a forward roll, ducking behind a parked car.

VoSkhar sent three bolts of energy out in rapid-fire succession. Mal and Sable both ducked.

Meanwhile, the inhabitants of the town square scattered.

The third bolt took out one of the legs of a nearby water tower.

The tower collapsed toward Sable's position.

Mal sent a bubble of magical energy to serve as a shield to protect Sable from the falling water tank.

VoSkhar took the opportunity and used a burst of energy to thrust Mal through a shop's plate glass window.

In her hidden location, Jenalee smiled. This was going according to her plan.

VoSkhar glanced about. The street stood nearly deserted.

At least, people had huddled behind cars and in shops.

VoSkhar noticed an old man hunched over and shuffling to a storefront doorway. The old man glanced over his shoulder. Terror on his face.

I'll give him something to fear, VoSkhar thought, and he changed into his Khodan demon-form.

Startled, the old man wobbled and fell to the ground. Then he feebly crawled to take refuge in the recess of a doorway.

At that moment, Khodan-VoSkhar decided to ignore this pathetic ant of a human being.

As soon as Khodan-VoSkhar turned his back, the old man held up his hand and sent a burst of energy that tossed Khodan-VoSkhar into the air.

Flailing about, Khodan-VoSkhar then hit hard on the asphalt of the street.

Seeing his moment, Jack with his AngelSword in hand made his move.

From the ground, Khodan-VoSkhar aimed an energy-hand at Jack. The fingers of the energy-hand turned into twenty hands all wielding razor-sharp short swords.

Using his AngelSword, Jack was a blur, blocking the attacks.

Slash. Jack got a cut on his right forearm.

Too many. Jack would soon fall to the twenty energy-hands swinging the swords.

Marta charged Khodan-VoSkhar. And he tossed her into a dumpster. He caused the dumpster lid to crash down, hitting her on the head. Marta did not rise her metal coffin.

The old man raised his hands and energy bolts fired upon VoSkhar from behind. Trin's smile grew wide and it cracked a bit of the old man's makeup she wore.

She felt great pride in smacking the demon Khodan with

some of his own medicine.

Sable Cane approached from Khodan-VoSkhar's left.

She joined Trin in slamming Khodan-VoSkhar with energy-bolts.

Trin glanced at Sable. This was strange.

Their combined might rammed Khodan-VoSkhar into a parked car then a lamp post.

Severely injured, Khodan rolled until his body became an inert mass near the corner of a building that was near an alleyway.

Sable saw her chance. She marched toward Khodan-VoSkhar.

Jenalee saw Sable's expression and felt the intuitive nudge that she had to stop Sable from getting near the Judas Gauntlet. Of course, Sable wanted the Obscurum, but she would be a greater foe than Mal. Where was Mal?

Jenalee threw her bolas. Sable barely raised her hand to stop the bolas from strangling her. The bolas ensnarled her hand and neck. Then Jenalee grabbed Sable. They both glowed, then fell through Achan Vortex, ending up in the Ninth Realm.

Sable and Jenalee found themselves on the grass.

Sable stirred and found herself floating up from the ground.

"Where are—?" Sable wondered.

"The Ninth Realm," Jenalee said.

"You really think you can hold me here, little Girlie?"

"Watch me," Jenalee said.

Jenalee kicked off a tree, and she zoomed toward and punched Sable Cane right in the face.

The impact cut Sable's upper lip on her incisor tooth. She touched her hand to her upper lip and noticed the blood on her forefinger. Her eyes flashed with fury.

She shrieked, "You, little bitch!" Her incisor teeth elongated. She aimed her hand in Jenalee's direction. No magical fireball issued forth. Sable grunted in frustration.

Chapter 50

As soon as Jenalee and Sable winked out from the earthly realm, Jack looked back at Khodan-VoSkhar's body, only to see Mal rip a bag that held the Cross of Sighs and Judas Gauntlet—from the inert demon's shoulder.

Mal sent an energy bolt, knocking Trin into a building's brick wall. She slid down. Unconscious.

Mal used both of his hands and sent two parked cars to form a sandwich that imprisoned Jack.

Mal opened the shoulder bag slung across his chest. He smiled. The Judas Gauntlet gleamed. Made of 30 pieces of silver. The price Judas Iscariot was paid to betray Jesus, the Christ.

He could feel the Judas Gauntlet pulsate with power. Sense it calling the other artifacts all going by the aggregate name, The Obscurum. First, the Cross of Sighs climbed out of the bag that Mal had taken from Khodan-VoSkhar.

Moving like a spider, The Cross of Sighs wrapped itself around the Judas Gauntlet.

Then, both glowing and floating, the Silent Scepter and Flute of Nightmares rose out of the mouth of the Mal's own bag. Both artifacts melded themselves onto the Judas Gauntlet.

Mal felt the call—as if the Sword of the Dark Bloom called out, *Release me.*

Mal put on the Judas Gauntlet. Feeling the new surge of

power, the Sword of the Dark Bloom slipped off unconscious Trin's back.

Once the Sword of the Dark Bloom arrived in Mal's posession, he pulled the Sword from its scabbard and raised the reunited Obscurum artifacts up and over his head.

The surrounding air crackled with energy. A smell of ozone permeated the air.

Noah raced up to Jack, still struggling to release himself from the parked-cars prison.

"It just gets better," Jack said.

Noah said, "Sometimes, Jack, I wish you'd stop saying that."

"Saying what?"

"Great. It's subconscious with you," Noah said.

Mal raised his right arm—the Judas Gauntlet now complete with the Cross of Sighs, Flute of Nightmares and Silent Scepter all melded into the artifact.

Seeing the Judas Gauntlet with the Sword of the Dark Bloom, all wielded by Mal, Noah shook his head and thought, *We're going to die.*

Chapter 51

Mal waved the Obscurum, a big smile on his face. "Jack ... too late again, brother."

Noah continued pulling on some twisted metal, trying to release Jack.

"Jack, what's going on? What about your AngelSword? To cut you free."

"I don't know. Maybe Mal put some kind of energy-dampening spell on these cars?" Jack said.

"This charade ends now. My wife will be restored to me," Mal said. "And this entire, disgusting timeline will be erased. Brother, we won't clash. We might never meet. And my wife never gets that horrific disease—"

"He's monologuing. Shouldn't we—?" Noah began.

"You're an idiot, Mal," Jack said. "You mess with the timeline like that. Then you don't even exist, and you won't be able to make your wishes come true," Jack said.

"And you're unenlightened," Mal said. "The Obscurum changes the fabric of reality. This is not some silly time travel routine. I can order anything. And I order ... Alicia restored to me."

Jack focused on Mal. Would his half-brother get what he wanted? How would Mal's upsetting the natural course of life throw the earth and the 9 Realms into chaos? Everything was connected.

Nothing happened.

Mal's eyes went wide. His voice hoarse as he said, "No! This is supposed to … I have the will to …"

Jack said, "Not really brother. Every evil act you've done. I'll bet that you've drained yourself of …"

Attempting to recover, Mal glanced at his injured hand—missing two fingers. "Restore my hand."

Instantly, Mal's two missing fingers materialized. He was healed.

Mal aimed the Obscurum at Jack, still stuck in the cars-sandwich with Noah struggling desperately to free his friend.

With a thought, Mal caused the Obscurum to issue a shockwave that tossed the cars-sandwich, with Jack within and Noah clinging on the outside, back fifty feet.

"Bow down before the power of the Obscurum. And I might let some of you live," Mal said, glancing at Jack, Noah and a couple of people running on the street.

"Somebody give this idiot a comic book to read. His lines are so bad," Noah said.

"I'll show you bad," Mal said. He wielded the Sword of the Dark Bloom and a pulsating beam of magical energy struck the Thomas Jefferson statue. At fourteen feet tall, the statue came to life and looked down upon Noah. Jack remained in the cars-sandwich. But the impact of the tossed cars had jarred the crumpled mass, so Jack began to free himself.

Noah stared, as the Thomas Jefferson statue stepped off its pedestal.

Jack said, "It's just gets—"

"You finish that sentence, and I'll slap you," Noah said.

The friends shared a smile.

Mal turned and sent another bolt of energy to awaken the companion statue, Benjamin Franklin, that adorned the other side of the quad.

Both statues grabbed cars and tossed them at Jack and Noah.

One car grazed the dumpster where Marta had been knocked unconscious.

The dumpster lid moved, as Marta freed herself. The Thomas Jefferson-statue tossed a car at her.

Marta Chang darted to the side. No way could that car strike her; she moved too fast. She tossed a newspaper dispenser immediately under the foot of the Thomas Jefferson statue. The Statue waivered and careened to the side just about to fall on Jack. He swung his AngelSword and sliced the statue in half, causing the portions to fall to either side of him.

Using his two firearms, Noah concentrated his fire on the Benjamin Franklin statue's right ankle. This caused the statue to topple over. On hitting the ground, the statue broke into five pieces. Neutralized.

Using the Obscurum, Mal conjured a huge hand made of oakwood. The tip of all five fingers formed as spears. Mal sent the oakwood at Marta who barely pivoted and avoided being impaled. Still, the oakwood hand impaled the lawn of the quad, creating an instant cage for Marta.

With her great strength, Marta kicked at the cage, but the enchanted wood did not budge.

Marta could not break free.

Jack raced forward, his AngelSword ready to do deadly damage to Mal.

Mal used the Obscurum to send out waves of energy that knocked Jack back fifteen feet into a wall of the local bank. Jack slid down the wall, out cold.

Trin swung on a rope of energy from Mal's right. She fired bolts of energy out of her left palm.

Mal cast a spell with the Obscurum, turning Trin's projected energy back on her. Using the Obscurum, Mal enchanted an old steel bumper from a classic truck. The bumper came alive and detached from the truck. The bumper sprouted spider legs and seized Trin, leaving her bundled. She was caught, like an immobilized fly in a web.

Chapter 52

"You did it, didn't you?" Jenalee said, facing down Sable in the 9th Realm.

"What?" Sable said, as she fumbled and held onto the branch of a tree to stabilize herself.

"You did something to the Obscurum," Jenalee surmised.

"What makes you think I did that?"

"I know you. Besides, you're smarter than Mal," Jenalee said.

"That's true." Sable smiled.

"What did you do?"

"What? Are you expecting me to tip my hand? Tell you all about my plans?" Sable asked. "That's amateur hour."

"And what about Daniel? You've been out of the InBetween, but you didn't go after Daniel."

Sable laughed.

It sounded weird to Jenalee. A choking sound.

"Some ... priorities change. You're not getting any hints from me, Little Girlie."

Sable grabbed a thin branch, broke it. Then she smiled seeing a sharp end. Now she had a weapon. Sable used her strong, toned legs to kick up and dart at Jenalee. Sable was now using the strange reduced gravity of the 9th Realm in her favor.

Using her skills borne of her practice sessions in the Adversary Room, Jenalee pivoted out of the way of Sable's weapon.

Sable twisted and then used her legs to entrap Jenalee.

Jenalee managed to knock the branch-weapon from Sable's hand, but simultaneously Sable pulled a switchblade, hidden inside a fold of her blouse.

Sable pressed the button, opening the blade. She jabbed the blade at Jenalee, who squirmed. Sable buried the blade in Jenalee's shoulder.

Jenalee did a palm strike into Sable's face.

Sable's legs loosened a bit. Jenalee took advantage of this and kicked the tree trunk, launching herself away from Sable.

Jenalee reached into her shoulder bag and pulled out a roll of duct tape.

Using her teeth, she pulled up the edge of the duct tape. She wrapped the shoulder and the blade to secure them. Wisely, she made the blade stay in her—to avoid bleeding out.

Jenalee kicked off a tree and launched herself at Sable. She twisted in mid-flight and kicked her opponent in the head.

Jenalee used duct tape to bind Sable's hands.

Sable kicked off of a tree and floated backward.

"I still have the use of my feet," Sable said.

Sable kicked off another tree in an attempt to rush Jenalee and hit her like a battering ram.

"You've think you've beaten me, Little Girlie?" Sable said.

"I am a woman. And you are nothing," Jenalee said.

Jenalee ducked and pulled a cord made of duct tape. This released a tree branch functioned like a trebuchet, which hit Sable square in the chest.

Sable fell backward, right into the gaping maw of a tunnel of energy leading to a gateway of the InBetween. Jenalee smiled to see that the trap she set using duct tape had done its job. At that moment, she recalled how she found a way to implement a strategic idea from Miyamoto Musashi: *You should not have a favorite weapon. To become over-familiar with one weapon is as much a fault as not knowing it sufficiently well.*

Seeing herself falling on a collision course back to the InBetween, Sable screamed and wailed in despair.

After swallowing Sable, the gateway to the InBetween snapped shut.

Chapter 53

Still in pain from the knife in her shoulder, Jenalee stepped out of the glowing ring—a portal from the 9th Realm to the Earth.

Mal saw Jenalee. He aimed the Obscurum, pointing the Sword of the Dark Bloom, and sent a bolt of energy that barely missed Jenalee as she as ducked out of the way. The bolt totaled a parked car.

Jenalee grunted in pain and gently pressed her wound area and to ascertain that the knife was still immobilized by the duct tape. It was.

Mal's eyebrows rose as he thought of a great way to kill this brat.

He aimed the Obscurum at a Cross at the top of a nearby church. The Cross bent forward as if bowing. For good measure, Mal directed the Obscurum to change reality and place a razor-sharp point at the top of the Cross.

Jenalee ducked behind various cars, making her way closer to Mal. He saw her reflection on a shop window. He aimed the Obscurum and lifted a car off the street, revealing Jenalee's hiding spot. His next blast of energy seized Jenalee as if she was caught in a mighty hand.

This energy hand lifted her up sixteen feet, and Jenalee caught sight of the Cross. She knew Mal's plans to impale her. *Hate this way to die*, Jenalee thought.

The energy hand threw her at the Cross.

Fifteen feet away.

Five feet.

The White Dragon's open claw caught Jenalee.

Jenalee looked to the White Dragon's face. "Nice catch."

"My pleasure."

Next to the White Dragon, a stunning Emerald Dragon let fly a torrent of fire-breath at Mal.

Mal barely made a magic shield, using the Obscurum. Somehow, although protected, he still felt the air near him heat up.

"Good shot," Jenalee said to the Emerald Dragon, who glistened in the sunlight.

"Thank you. I know you are Jenalee. Call me Emmy," the Emerald Dragon said.

"Drengard—" Jenalee said, expressing the White Dragon's real name. "That was good timing—your catching me."

"I taught him that," Emmy said. She laughed, and Jenalee joined her.

White Dragon skipped his retort and sent another fire-blast at Mal.

Jack shook his head, trying to come back to being fully alert. He saw the special group of people that he had directed Mrs. Chi to use as the "special backup plan."

Mal's attention remained fully occupied by the double assault of the two fire-breathing dragons. Still, Mal remained in his position on a pedestal above a fountain—with a water pool in front of him.

Jack guided the special group of people to take their positions and accomplish their task.

Jack nodded to Jenalee.

Jenalee stealthily approached Mal from the side. In one

motion, Jenalee pressed the button on her bladed-fighting stick to have the blade go into position—while she swiftly jumped to the pedestal Mal stood on.

With all her might, Jenalee swung down her bladed fighting stick, severing Mal's arm at the shoulder. The arm, encased in the Judas Gauntlet with the hand holding the Sword of the Dark Bloom, fell into the fountain water.

At that moment, Jenalee could hear the assembled holy people including priests and priestesses chanting and praying.

Jenalee prayed, too—hoping that the water now blessed and made holy by these clergy could neutralize the Obscurum.

Upon hitting the water, the Obscurum lost its unholy light, extinguished like a candle's flame.

Jenalee felt a percussive shockwave, permeating the area surrounding the fountain. It was as if all of creation acknowledged that a great thing had just happened.

People from so many places across the world united to extinguish the influence of pure evil.

Exuberance rolled like a benevolent tidal wave through the people. The Rabbi playfully jabbed the Christian priest. They laughed in sheer joy. The Buddhist monk bowed to the middle-eastern spiritual leader, who bowed back. They smiled.

Jack's mentor, Tanaka, who was also a Taoist priest, strode over to Jack and shook his hand.

Then Jack saw something he never saw before Noah hugged Tanaka. Father and son, at least for the moment, comfortable in each other's presence.

Members of nature religions hugged each other with exclamations of "Blessed Be!"

The cage of oakwood dissolved into nothing, and Marta

was free. She moved as fast as lightning, and hugged Jack.

Trin tapped Marta on the shoulder. Marta took a step back and Trin got in a hug with Jack, too.

Noah dashed over to Jenalee. In joy, Noah moved to hug her, but he saw the duct-taped switchblade in her shoulder.

"That's got to hurt," Noah said.

She leaned toward him, smiling anyway.

They kissed.

Mrs. Chi used magical spells to keep Mal contained even as Helios personnel dealt with Mal's wounds. Then Mrs. Chi made sure that Mal was stowed in a brig cell that she had pre-treated. She had used seven magical spells to serve as containment fields for Mal.

Jack decided to cool down from the final fight by taking a walk on the SkyLevel.

That was where Marta found him.

They walked side by side.

"You know, Jack." Marta said, "Trin's heart is on the line. It's clear: She wants you to choose her."

"I know," Jack said.

"You might say that because I live so long that it would be only fair that I step aside."

Marta looked into Jack's eyes. She said, "I'm *not* that noble."

Marta held up a bracelet for Jack.

"What's that?"

"Let's say that this is a keepsake to celebrate our triumph against Mal, Sable, and Khodan," Marta said, a twinkle in her eye. Mrs. Chi's team had searched for Khodan-VoSkhar but he was gone.

Jack eyed the bracelet in Marta's hand and asked, "It's not

some bonding ritual or something, right?"

"It's not. Unless you want to add to it," Marta said.

"Well ... I ..."

Marta moved as a blur.

Jack patted his right trousers pocket.

"The bracelet is in my pocket, right?"

"Something for a rainy day, Jack," Marta said.

Chapter 54

"Jack, you know this is going to be cruel," Noah said, glancing at Jack—as they prepared for the next event.

Jack shrugged into a pressed dress shirt as he glanced about his cabin on board the Helios.

"What?" Jack asked.

"You know what."

"Oh, you mean, I got to declare myself as with Marta or with Trin?"

Noah nodded.

Anguish came upon Jack's face. "I don't know. I care about them both. I'm attracted to both of them. And I know that they want me to choose. I really don't know what to do."

Jack buttoned his shirt as they were getting ready for dinner with the other members of Jenalee's team.

"What are you doing?

"What?" Jack asked.

"You're wearing the bracelet from Marta and the belt buckle from Trin. Are you crazy?"

"What would you have me do?"

"Not get killed."

"What?"

"They'll hate each other. They'll hate you. They might plot your death together!"

"I think you're—"

"Sensible. Aware," Noah said. "You think I could wear something from another woman with Jenalee looking on?

"You're a couple."

"And you're a nut! I'm trying to save you from being a dead nut."

"Maybe I can talk to them. They're both my friends.

"What? Together?" Noah asked, aghast.

"It's what adults do."

"You academia types. Got a problem? Throw a bunch of words at it."

A knock at the door.

Jack had trouble closing the bracelet clasp on the gift from Marta.

The doorknob turned.

Marta and Trin were stopping by.

They started to enter the room.

Noah faked that he fainted — as he fell over, Noah pulled the bracelet off Jack's wrist.

"Noah! Are you okay?" Trin asked.

"Uh. Just fine. Didn't eat breakfast," Noah said.

"Do we have to carry you?" Marta said. She glanced at Jack's wrists to see if he wore her bracelet.

Seated at the dinner table, Jack looked around and noticed the delegates — the leaders from various religious groups. They had all participated in thwarting the Obscurum. As a former comparative religion college instructor, Jack had the idea to gather leaders from various spiritual paths. Their combined efforts would ensure that the water would transform into holy water to neutralize the Obscurum. Cooperation won the day.

Jack noticed that Trin glanced over to see he wore the magical belt buckle that she gave him. He didn't know whether it had magical properties, but the symbols on it gave him the impression that there might be more to this gift.

Trin smiled.

Jack thought, *What am I going to do? Now, she thinks that I'm hers.*

Marta glanced at Jack. He could tell that Marta had observed how Trin liked that Jack wore her gift for him

Jack looked at Marta. She gave him a special smile. And then she tilted her head in a move that was so inviting and sexy.

Moved, Jack glanced around and had a drink of ice water.

After the dinner came to a close, Jack returned to his room. He picked up his cell phone and dialed.

"Hi, Mom."

The next morning, Jack found Jenalee walking on the track at the SkyLevel.

"I'm fine. Really," Jenalee said into her cell phone.

"You always sound out of breath when you call and check in on me," Marina said on her side of the phone call.

Jenalee felt a warm connection with this high school student she had tutored for a year—all in the efforts to help Marina be the first in her family to go to college.

"I'm on the move a lot," Jenalee said. "I travel. So, what are you learning with Ms. Ahlei?"

Marina told Jenalee about a couple of new studying techniques Ms. Ahlei gave her.

In a couple of moments, Jenalee and Marina brought their phone conversation to a close.

"You're doing well, Marina. I'm proud of you—by that I mean—"

"You're celebrating my progress—I know," Marina said. She and Jenalee chuckled.

Jack walked up to Jenalee. He noticed that Jenalee's blouse puffed out where the bandages on her shoulder were.

Walking at her side, he said, "You're a great leader. You led me. You're my mentor."

Minutes later, Jenalee found Noah having breakfast at the Grand Hall.

"You all right?" Noah asked Jenalee.

"I'm good," she said. "I think I finally got what my Gram-Gram tried to tell me over the years: *Show up to each moment fresh.*"

"Does it mean something different to you now?" Noah asked.

"A lot. I don't have the words. But I know that I feel it in my gut," Jenalee said.

She turned and pulled Noah close.

Jenalee and Noah kissed.

A good kiss.

No, a great kiss.

A kiss to break the Internet.

Jenalee felt her heart fill up. *This moment. I'm doing well. I feel strong.*

Now that you've read Novel #2 of the *Jenalee Storm Trilogy* ...
Read the Whole Trilogy:

Excerpt from the 3rd Novel in this *Jenalee Storm Trilogy*

Chapter 1

Death mocked me from the lifeless eyes of the woman whose essence had been drained from her neck. My grandmother had said, "Jenalee, often the deadly kiss of a vampire is part of an ecstatic ancient ritual." Over the centuries, many willing victims longed for the orgasmic experience uniquely provided by a vampire's feeding.

But this woman's face was a stark contrast. The sheer agony frozen on her face knocked me back, hitting my shoulders on a wall. This was no ordinary vampire's feeding. It was something else.

Terror. Agony. Something profoundly evil had done this.

A dead body was my first problem. My second problem was I didn't know where I was or how I had ended up in this room on the floor with a corpse.

I struggled to my knees. This room? I saw a window—no,

a porthole. A view of the turbulent, dark sea. A flash of lightning.

I'm on a ship!

My eyes strayed to the woman's right hand. Her hand remained in a death grip on the comforter dragged off the bed.

And my last memory was my mentor, Jack AngelSword, gripping my forearm.

Jack AngelSword held my forearm, with urgency. "Jenalee, there's something off here. It would be—"

That's when I saw two opponents, guns at the ready. They pushed through the thick foliage, making their way toward us— from the left.

Letting go of my forearm, Jack saw those guys plus another two coming from another direction.

Crouching and with stealth, I dashed forward to surprise the two opponents before me.

Automatic gunfire broke a tree branch that hit Jack AngelSword on the head. He fell back unconscious into a nearby rowboat. That jostled the boat to enter a current of the river. The boat and river began taking Jack away.

I ran at top speed; then I jumped and landed in the boat. That's when I found our boat commandeered by the current of a waterfall just yards away.

We are going to go over the waterfall in seconds and die. Maybe, I could pull Jack off the boat. Then I'd have to try to keep him afloat. Years ago, I hadn't passed the Lifesaver test when I was 14, and they had me try to save somebody that weighed 120 pounds more than I did. I failed then. And, this felt like a crappy recreation of that situation.

No—it was too late already. We were nine feet from the edge with the water plunging over the cliff!

A glowing young woman rose from just beyond the edge of the waterfall. She aimed her right hand and sent a magical force-beam that pushed the boat into a cove. She saved us.

She had the boat rise then rest on dry land.

The next moment, she gracefully floated to us and landed in the boat. She tapped Jack on his shoulder.

She was a Latina, slender, attractive. Her long hair that draped past her waist fluttered in the wind, resembling a cape. "Wake up, Jack."

"You know, Jack?" I asked.

"I'm Nia. I'm his sister."

"Wait—what?"

Then I smiled. "You're Jack's sister. I'm his student. That makes us—"

Nia frowned. "Strangers."

I shook my head. I reached for my usual holsters for my fighting sticks. Oh, good. My fighting sticks were there.

Got to my feet. Other than that memory of Jack and Nia, I had no memory of how I got to this ship. This had to be trouble.

Grabbed one fighting stick with my right hand, at the ready for anything or anyone that could come through the cabin door.

In our last battle with VoSkhar, we had soundly defeated him, but he had managed to slink away. As both the head of the House of Dagger and a freaking demon, his next steps would likely be horrific. Outlandish and effective. Plus he's a damn shapeshifter.

I didn't know any shapeshifter who was trustworthy. Even Gram-Gram's cat, Magic, was a shapeshifter. But he wasn't trustworthy. He had abandoned me on the street when we had gone for groceries. Soon after, another shapeshifter—the asshole werewolf Erik had nearly killed me.

Magic had strayed away, leaving me without an ally.

But then I remembered his face—in his human form. When he had heard about what happened, he had looked stricken.

Could a cat be ashamed of himself?

... he's not really a cat. Just some magical creature—or person—who shifts from housecat form to ... to ... why did he have to be so gorgeous?

Yeah. Well, pretty doesn't mean good.

End of Excerpt – Novel 3 of *The Dark Crossing Trilogy*.

Also by Raven Aren James
Read the Whole Trilogy … and Continue the Journey:

Jenalee Storm and her mentor, Jack AngelSword, face a whole universe of vampires, werewolves, demons, dragons and unspeakable evil.

Here's your chance to get access to **Behind-the-Scenes fun.** When you **subscribe** to the exclusive enewsletter:

• **See Exclusive Artwork** (from the upcoming graphic novels)
• **Discover details** about movement toward a television series and/or feature films
• **Get Early Access** to announcements about upcoming books, graphic novels, merchandise and more related to Jenalee Storm and her friends.

Subscribe at JenaleeStorm.com/subscribe

ABOUT THE AUTHOR

Raven Aren James is an author, screenwriter and feature film director. Some of Raven's work appears under different pen names.

"If you enjoyed this novel, would you consider posting a sentence or two and share your honest opinion of this book?

When new readers see a good list of reviews, they will find me. Each review means so much to me. Thank you for reading *Jenalee Storm: Magic Endures."* – Raven Aren James